THUNDER ON FORBIDDEN MOUNTAIN

WESTMINSTER PRESS BOOKS BY

THEODORE W. MUNCH
Man the Engineer—Nature's Copycat

THEODORE W. MUNCH AND ROBERT D. WINTHROP
Thunder on Forbidden Mountain

THUNDER ON FORBIDDEN MOUNTAIN

by
Theodore W. Munch
and
Robert D. Winthrop

The Westminster Press
Philadelphia

COPYRIGHT © 1976
THEODORE W. MUNCH AND ROBERT D. WINTHROP

All rights reserved—no part of this book may be reproduced in any form without permission in writing from the publisher, except by a reviewer who wishes to quote brief passages in connection with a review in magazine or newspaper.

BOOK DESIGN BY DOROTHY E. JONES

PUBLISHED BY THE WESTMINSTER PRESS ®
PHILADELPHIA, PENNSYLVANIA

PRINTED IN THE UNITED STATES OF AMERICA

Library of Congress Cataloging in Publication Data

Munch, Theodore W
   Thunder on Forbidden Mountain.

   SUMMARY: Kevin, his sister Marcy, and Apache "sitter" Ramona take a tenderfoot Ohio cousin on a long hike into the Superstition Mountains of Arizona where they encounter more adventure than they anticipated.
   [1. Arizona—Fiction. 2. Adventure stories. 3. Indians of North America—Fiction] I. Winthrop, Robert D., 1932–   joint author. II. Title.
PZ7.M92327Th   [Fic]   75–35852
ISBN 0–664–32588–2

To children the world over
>who love a good adventure story.
>>T.W.M.

>To my mother, my son,
Sean,
>>and to my coauthor,
>>>who believed I could.
>>>>R.D.W.

CONTENTS

1	Cousin Trouble	9
2	A Close Call	16
3	Wee-Kit-Saur-Ah	28
4	Apache Revenge	34
5	A Cave and Some Cobs	40
6	The Lost Dutchman?	46
7	Jake Disappears	52
8	Look Before You Leap!	59
9	Watch That First Step!	65
10	The Thunder Gods Lend a Hand	74
11	Beware of Falling Rocks	83
12	Prisoner of War	89
13	Dry Bones	98
14	Escape at Night	106
15	Through the Looking Glass	116
16	Brig Drops out of Sight	125
17	Light at the End of the Tunnel	129
18	Thunder in the Superstitions	137
19	Big Bird from the Sky	148
	To Our Readers	155

1
COUSIN TROUBLE

Darby Driscoll stood in the dark hallway peering into his cousin's room. Kevin Coleman stood before a long mirror studying the reflection of a crinkled map that he held in his hands.

What on earth is he doing? Darby thought. Looks like he's been out in the blasted Arizona sun too long today and it fried his brain.

Darby continued to watch as Kevin, tracing a line on the map, followed the movement of his finger in the mirror.

Unable to contain his curiosity any longer, Darby walked into Kevin's room. "It's finally happened," he said. "You've really flipped your lid."

Startled, Kevin turned to face his cousin, trying to conceal the map behind him. "No use trying to hide that map," said Darby. "I already saw it. What do you think you're doing, anyway?"

Kevin tried to look sheepish. "Well, I wasn't gonna show you, but I guess I'll have to now. Come here."

Kevin dropped to his knees and spread the map on the

carpet. "Ever hear of the Lost Dutchman Mine?" he asked.

"Sure," said Darby. "Who hasn't?"

"Well, this is a copy of the map that someone gave Larry to show him where to find petroglyphs. I think it may contain the secret of the Lost Dutchman Mine."

Larry, Kevin's brother, was nineteen and had just finished his sophomore year at Arizona State University. For one of his projects as an archaeology major, he had hiked into the nearby Superstition Mountains to search for petroglyphs, inscriptions made on rocks by early Indians.

"While I was looking over the map," Kevin went on, "I discovered some strange markings on it. Like this one." He pointed to what looked like an F. "If you hold the map up to a mirror, that F looks like a 7 with a line drawn across it, the way Europeans make a 7."

"What difference does that make?" asked Darby. "What if it is a 7? What does the 7 mean?"

Kevin pointed to some lines on the map that indicated a tall peak. "Well, it could mean that where the shadow of Weaver's Needle falls at seven o'clock is where the mine is located. And see this mark? When you hold it up to a mirror, it becomes an S. The S could mean south."

"Hey!" Darby looked more closely at the map. "You know, you may just have something. Look at this mark. What's it look like in the mirror?"

Kevin stood and held the map while the two boys examined the strange markings in the reflection. "Wow! It's a 40," Darby shouted. "It must mean you walk forty feet from this point."

"Could be," agreed Kevin. "But it could mean you have to dig forty feet down, too."

"Yeah, I guess you're right," said Darby. "I'll bet if we went there, though, we could be sure. Why don't we get someone to drive us into the mountains and see if your theory is right? We could get rich."

Kevin smiled. "In the first place, you can't even begin to drive into the Superstitions. And in the second place, we have to stick around here until Saturday, and then we're gonna drive up and meet Larry when he hikes out of the mountains."

Darby's excitement faded. "Yeah? Well, I never believed all that claptrap about the Lost Dutchman anyway. I think it's something the chamber of commerce cooked up to get more tourists to come to Arizona." With that he stomped out of the room and returned to the den to watch television.

Kevin watched his cousin go and then slowly folded the map and placed it in his desk drawer. Leaving his room, he walked down the hall, through the house, and out onto the front porch. His shoulders slumped in sadness. He was greeted by a small shaggy black dog.

"Hi, Brig," said Kevin, glumly sitting down on the steps. "How can you see with your hair always over your eyes like that?"

Brigadoon, a cairn terrier, waited for a friendly pat on the head, but when it was not forthcoming, he stretched out, his chin on his front paws, and looked sadly up at Kevin.

From where he sat, Kevin gazed past the neighbors' houses at the Superstitions, which lay to the east of the town Apache Junction. The play of shadows from the clouds caused the mountains to change colors almost constantly.

At one moment an area appeared dark and brooding, and then, as the clouds moved, the same peak or canyon broke into sunlight and almost glistened in brilliance. What a great place I live in! he thought, trying to be more cheerful.

As he sat thinking, a huge cloud shadow covered the mountains, and Kevin's gloom returned. He tried to figure

11

out what had gone wrong with the summer. For months he had looked forward to the arrival of Darby from Ohio. A hundred times he had thought how great it would be to have someone his own age staying with him. He had fixed up his room and made a list of activities he thought would keep two boys busy for months. But now, at the end of two weeks, he had lost all enthusiasm for trying to entertain his cousin.

From the minute Darby had arrived at the Phoenix airport, Kevin had liked him. Darby, tall, blond, and gangly, had kept the whole family laughing with his funny stories about Ohio and with the way he acted them out with wild motions and weird facial expressions. But after a few days Darby ran out of new stories and he began to repeat the old ones.

It was Darby's bragging that bothered Kevin. Each item that he showed Darby met with instant disapproval because they had better ones in the Buckeye State. When he showed Darby his rifle, his cousin had said, "Oh, I've got two rifles back in Ohio." While Kevin had a three-speed bike, Darby had a ten-speed. It was all pretty frustrating.

Darby had asked, "Where are the cowboys?" and Kevin had taken him into downtown Apache Junction, which was spread along the highway. To be sure, several of the men they had seen dressed in Western clothes might have been businessmen or truck drivers, but a few of them, Kevin knew, were real working cowhands. He had even introduced Darby to a couple of cattlemen who were friends of his father, but Darby decided that since they weren't wearing six-shooters, they weren't real, honest-to-goodness cowboys.

As for Indians, didn't they have a real Apache staying with them for the summer as a live-in baby-sitter? Her name was Ramona Three Feathers, and she could speak Apache and sing Indian songs, and she knew all sorts of Indian legends. But Ramona preferred pantsuits to doeskin dresses, and she wore her long black hair in a ponytail rather than in braids, so Darby never quite believed she was a real Indian.

Ramona had promised to take them to visit her parents on the reservation as soon as Kevin's mother and father returned from their trip to Hawaii. Mr. Coleman had won the vacation for being the outstanding salesman in his district, and they had been gone for a week, leaving Ramona in charge until Larry returned. But until they could go to the reservation, Kevin was at a loss for things to do to entertain Darby, who didn't even pretend to be having a good time since his aunt and uncle's departure. He complained that the weather was too hot and spent most of his time watching television quiz shows. He said that the mountains didn't look the way he thought they would. He said that they should have snow on top and that there should be pine trees and white aspens.

Darby declared that the desert was ugly. He had expected sand dunes and swaying palm trees. The Arizona desert, he said, should be given back to the rattlesnakes and gila monsters. But most often he went back to his old story that the West wasn't what he had expected. Movies and television had succeeded not in opening doors but in closing Darby's mind.

Feeling thirsty, Kevin went in to the kitchen, where he found Ramona talking to his little sister, Marcy. After getting a drink of water from the refrigerator, he silently joined them at the table.

"What's wrong?" asked Ramona. "More cousin trouble?"

"Something like that," said Kevin. "I wish I could think of something interesting for us to do."

"I think I know a way you can keep Darby busy for a while," said Ramona, her dark eyes shining.

"How?" asked Kevin, not showing much interest.

"How!" said Ramona, laughing and putting her hand up in mock Indian fashion.

"Oh, I thought you were serious," groaned Kevin, starting to rise from the table.

Ramona put her hand on his arm. "I'm sorry," she said. "I know you have troubles, but I really do have an idea. How would you like for the four of us to hike out and meet Larry where he's working, rather than just pick him up as we had planned?"

"I don't know," said Kevin. "That's pretty rough country, and I'm not sure you guys could make it. It's awfully hot, and that's a lot of hiking."

"What do you mean?" asked Marcy, finally speaking up. "Didn't I make the ten-mile hike with the Dons in March?" The Dons were a group of Arizona men interested in preserving the legends and lore of Arizona. Each year they took guided tours into the Superstitions. "I can make it if you can. Besides, I think it will be fun."

"Don't worry about me either, you male chauvinist," laughed Ramona. "I may be a little overweight, but these little short legs of mine have been all over the Apache reservation chasing cattle and sheep. I'll keep up with you."

"Yeah, but what about Darby?" asked Kevin. "He's never been out in the desert very much, and he might really slow us down."

"Well," answered Ramona, "we won't be going till day after tomorrow. Why don't we take him hiking tomorrow and see how he does? We can take him up to Goldfields. That ought to be a good test."

Kevin came to life. "Great!" he exclaimed. "I'll go tell ol' Darb now. I'll bet this'll get him away from the television."

Soon Kevin was explaining to Darby about their proposed plans. Darby was less than enthusiastic about so much walking in the hot Arizona sun. "Marcy was right, I guess," fibbed Kevin. "She sorta wondered if an Eastern dude could keep up with the rest of us."

This statement brought Darby to his feet. "You mean she's going? Why, she'll melt out there, and all they'll find is a little puddle."

"Are you kidding?" asked Kevin. "She can hike twenty miles and still be rarin' to go. I'll admit we'll be going over some pretty rough ground, though."

Kevin reached into his back pocket and pulled out the map that he had shown to Darby earlier. He spread it out on the carpet. "Let me show you our route. We'll leave the jeep here." He pointed to a spot on the map. "Then we'll go up here. And camp along about here."

Darby's eyes followed Kevin's finger as it traced its way along a dotted line, but then he was distracted by more strange markings he had not seen before.

"Don't worry about me," Darby said. "Just 'cause I'm from the East doesn't mean that I'm a tenderfoot. I've done some hiking too, you know."

"Oh, I don't doubt that," Kevin assured him. "But since we have some time before Saturday, we're gonna go on a little shakedown hike tomorrow, just to be sure that we know what we're getting into."

"Sounds fine to me," replied Darby. "Say, could you leave that map with me for a while? I'd like to see if I can decipher some more of those marks. I still don't think there's any gold out there, but it might be kinda fun to look around a little."

"Sure," said Kevin, a smile forming on his lips as he handed the map to his cousin. "Keep it all night if you want. See you later."

2

A CLOSE CALL

The alarm was very loud and very steady. A brown hand snaked out from under the sheet, but it couldn't seem to find the clock. The arm attached to the hand made one big swoop and the clock crashed to the floor. From somewhere under the sheet there came a groan, and another arm and a tousled head joined the first arm as Kevin's body leaned over the edge of the bed. He scooped up the clock and punched the alarm button into silence.

"Oh, no," groaned Kevin. "It can't be time to get up yet." Suddenly, Kevin's mind started working rapidly. Today was the shakedown hike to make sure that all was in readiness for the three-day trip into the Superstitions.

Kevin raised his legs and placed the soles of his feet on the bulge that was above him in the top bunk. He pushed hard a few times and the bump bounced up and down. A second later a muffled voice grumbled, "What in the heck is going on? It's too early to get up yet."

"Oh, no, Darby, out of the sack," Kevin chuckled. He started playing a tattoo on the bump, which shifted its position, moaned again, and fell into silence.

"Hey," exclaimed Kevin. "Up . . . up. We have lots to do today."

"Okay, okay, already," Darby grunted. "I'm coming down. Watch out below!" Two feet appeared over the edge of the bunk, and the rest of the body half fell and half jumped to the floor. Darby stood by the bed, yawned loudly, scratched his head, and peered at Kevin through barely open eyes. "I hope you're satisfied," he said.

"Just had to make sure you were up. Why don't you use the bathroom first while I toss my bed together?"

Darby shuffled off, slammed the door, and started running the water. Kevin shrugged his shoulders, turned back to the bed, threw the covers over it, and hurried into his jeans, Western shirt, and ankle-high hiking boots. A few minutes later, he had washed and was accompanying Darby to the kitchen.

Ramona greeted them with a soft smile and a quiet, "Hi! Are you guys hungry? The cereal and milk are out, the toast is in the oven, and the cocoa will be ready in a few minutes."

"I don't know about Darby, but I'm starving," replied Kevin as he slid into his seat by the window.

Darby only scowled, but his juice disappeared in about two gulps.

Marcy bounced into the kitchen, tucking her shirt into her jeans. "Gosh, thanks for waiting, guys."

"Don't worry, Marcy, there is more toast in the oven and extra cocoa on the stove," Ramona soothed. When the others had been served, she sat down, and for a while, only the crunching of food could be heard. The sun was just coming over the mountains that loomed in the distance. The ominous dark clouds of the night before had given way to fluffy white patches that cast shadows on the faces of the buff-colored cliffs. The rocks had a clean glow, and the green fields stretching up to the base of the cliffs seemed to be an inviting emerald road.

Darby broke the silence. "I don't see why we had to get up so early. It's just getting light outside."

"You'll be glad later for an early start," Kevin shot back. "It gets pretty hot hiking up those trails about noontime. We'd like to stop as often as we need to and still get in a pretty good day's hike."

"How far are we going today?" Darby inquired.

"About five or six miles, round trip," Marcy chipped in.

"Great Scott, five or six miles! I'm not sure that I want to try to go that far." Darby sounded just a bit whiny.

"Darb, here in the West, six miles isn't really much at all," Kevin teased. "Besides, there are so many interesting things to see, you won't notice how tired you are until you get back home."

"Well, maybe," Darby grumbled. "And I'm not sure that I like you calling me Darb. My name's Darby."

"Well, 'an even swap, and an even trade. My old gal for your old maid.'" Kevin smiled. "I'll go along with Kev, if I can call you Darb."

Ramona didn't give Darby a chance to answer. "Time is a-wasting," she said. "We have to get outside and lay out our gear. Darby, in the carport you'll find the box of supplies your folks sent out. Why not bring it around under the paloverde tree by the side of the house?"

Soon all four were busy placing their hiking equipment out on the ground and checking back and forth with each other to see that nothing was missing.

Kevin joined Darby and suggested that they check his gear. "Let's see. Sleeping bag, socks, Levi's, boots, canteen, Band-Aids, snakebite kit—"

"Snakebite kit?" Darby broke in with a startled voice.

"Will we really need that?"

"Man, I wouldn't be caught dead without a snakebite kit if I were going out on the desert or into the Superstitions this time of year." Kevin sounded very serious. "There are plenty of rattlers around, and the warm weather in June keeps them moving about quite a bit."

"Have you ever had to use it?" Darby's voice had risen.

"Not me, but I did see it used once when I was on a scout hike. A friend wandered off the trail and was struck in the leg," Kevin replied.

"Was he very sick?" Darby sounded a bit uneasy.

"I'll say he was," said Marcy. "He was in bed for three days. The doctor had to give him two antivenom shots."

"He probably wouldn't have lived at all," Kevin added, "if the scoutmaster hadn't used the snakebite kit right away. Let's see now," Kevin went back to checking gear. "You have your poncho, backpack, and flashlight. Do you have some extra batteries?"

"Everything's here as far as I can see," Darby replied.

"Let's check out your food supplies," suggested Ramona, who had been busy with her own checklist up to now.

"Looks as though I have more food than I have gear," Darby complained. "There is one good thing, though, most of the food is freeze-dried and doesn't weigh much."

"You'll be glad for that after the first few miles," Ramona smiled.

"Do I have to take everything?" Darby inquired with a note of dissatisfaction.

"No. You are the boss, but you may want to carry it all on the long trip, so you had better get used to the feel of it today," Ramona reminded him.

Darby called out the items in a low voice. "Pork chops, stew, bacon and eggs, orange drink, candy drops, crackers, some bread and butter, and ice cream. Ice cream? Freeze-dried ice cream? Someone is putting me on." Darby scowled and looked at Kevin.

"No, that's the real stuff," Kevin replied. "It's a gift for today's lunch from Marcy and me."

"What's it like?"

"Like dried ice cream. Sweet and fun to eat. You'll like it and want more," Marcy told him.

"I'd like to put in some tea," Darby said.

"Fine with us," Kevin replied. "We're taking some."

Ramona rose from her pile of gear and tossed a small can onto Darby's poncho. "Everybody has to carry some of the common property," she told Darby. "This is a can of butane for our primus stove. I'll be carrying the stove, and Kev and Marcy each have another can of gas. I have a map, Kevin has a rope, and Marcy will carry the packets of dry dog food for Brigadoon."

"Are you really taking the dog along?" Darby asked. "He doesn't look like much of a dog to go on a pack trip. His legs are too short, and he seems to be panting all the time."

"Hey, just a minute," Kevin shot back. "I'll have you know that Brig is a cairn terrier, bred for these sorts of things. His legs may be short, but they can keep going all day long, and he can dig for rabbits. You won't have to wait for him."

"Well, okay, but don't ask me to carry him if he gets stuck in a rock pile someplace," Darby grumbled.

Ramona reminded them that they ought to get on with the checking. "Who has the survival kit?"

"It's under my poncho, right here," Kevin told her.

"Survival kit? It sure sounds as though you're expecting one disaster after another. First a snakebite kit and now a survival thing. What's it used for?" Darby sounded a bit scared. "Sure isn't very big. Looks like a plastic sandwich box."

Kevin was happy to explain. "It doesn't look like much,

but every piece can help save your life if you are stranded in the desert. A small knife for cutting into a cactus. Some matches dipped in paraffin, and a small piece of candle to help save matches."

Kevin continued, holding up a large needle. "You can use this for sewing clothes or removing cactus spines. The one-edged razor blade can make incisions in case of snakebite, the tablets kill germs in water, and the aluminum foil is for signaling or cooking. You know what the antiseptic is for. Last, but not least, a small mirror."

"What's the mirror for?" Darby inquired.

"Marcy uses it to comb her hair in the morning," Kevin teased.

"Oh, come on," said Marcy. "Darby, we can use the mirror for sending light signals in case we are lost. Someone might see the flashing mirror and come help us."

A little while later, all the gear was stacked on the racks on the back of the jeep. Ramona was in the driver's seat with Marcy on her right. The two boys were perched on the back seat, waiting expectantly for the start of the engine. Brigadoon, sniffing the wind and eager to start, was held by Kevin.

Fifteen minutes later the jeep had pulled off the road and onto a trail that led up toward the Superstitions. When the trail became too rough, Ramona pulled the jeep over to one side, jumped out, and announced, "End of the line . . . everybody out!"

The party unloaded the gear, each one strapped on his pack, and then all waited until Ramona was ready to guide them up the trail. The hike started at Goldfields, near the Bluebird gold mine. The mine was no longer worked, but it was a tourist attraction for visitors from the East. The trail out of Goldfields sloped gently up toward the fortresslike hulks of the mountains. It was easy walking as Ramona led the way. Everybody had a neatly stacked pack—except Darby, that is.

About half an hour up the trail, he brought the column to an abrupt halt exclaiming, "Hey, my bedroll is gone!"

Kevin retrieved the roll and showed Darby how to restack the material on his backpack, and soon the line was moving again.

"I don't see why I need to carry that doggoned bedroll, anyway. It sure wasn't cold last evening, and I can't see it getting much colder in the mountains." This came from Darby as he stumbled over a rock in the path.

Ramona swung off the trail about half an hour later and slipped off her pack. She searched through one of the pockets, found a map, and after unfolding it beckoned to Darby. "I guess it's about time to show you how to get around by using a 'topo' map."

"I'm not sure what 'topo' means." Darby wore a quizzical expression.

"It's short for topographical. This map shows the roads, trails, the mountains, and canyons. It also shows some of the things man has put on the land, like ranches and mines. Notice all the brown lines running like spaghetti around the map? Each line connects points on the ground that are all the same height above sea level. Where the elevation lines are far apart, the ground slopes more or less gently. When the lines are jammed close together, there is a steep cliff or wall."

"I see." Darby was thoughtful. "I also see that the squares on this map are a mile on a side, if I'm reading the scale at the bottom correctly."

Ramona seemed a little amazed at Darby's quickness to catch on. I must have struck on something he likes, she thought to herself. "You are so right, Darby. Why not carry the map for a while? I want to drop back and talk to Kevin for a few minutes. We'll be going as far as First Water, but that's over a mile up the way. Do you see that big chunk of rock in the distance?"

"Couldn't miss it," answered Darby. He seemed to be a little taller now that he had assumed the lead position. "Looks like a big book being pushed out of the earth."

"Not a bad comparison," Ramona said. "If you look on the map, you'll see that it's called Weaver's Needle. The Spanish used to call it El Sombrero, because at certain angles it looks like a huge Mexican hat. It's the biggest landmark around here, and if you keep it on your left, you probably won't get lost."

Darby did a great job leading the column until he decided to stop and get a better look at the top of a towering saguaro cactus.

"How tall is this monster, anyway?" he asked.

"Must be at least twenty-five feet," Kevin responded. "Do you have any idea how old this cactus is?"

"Heck, no. Is there some way of telling just by looking? Wouldn't you have to cut one down and count the rings inside?" asked Darby.

"A cactus doesn't have rings, like a pine or an oak tree," Marcy explained. "But we do know that this kind of cactus grows only about one to two inches a year."

"And if you knew how many inches tall the cactus was, you could figure out the age by dividing the height by two inches a year. Let's see, now. If this one is twenty-five feet tall, that is the same as three hundred inches. That divided by two inches per year makes the cactus about 150 years old!" The arithmetic response came quickly from Darby.

"Nice going, Darb," Kevin said. He noticed that Darby didn't seem to mind the shorter nickname.

"Yeah, not bad, even if I do say so myself, Kev," Darby came back with a twinkle in his eye. "What are those things on the top part?" Darby slowly stepped backward, all the while looking up at the creamy yellow flowers that bedecked the top of the plant. Suddenly he halted and then leaped forward with a loud shout.

"Oh, oh, Darb, you sure did it this time," Marcy cried, running forward. "Stand still and stop thrashing about. You are just going to get the spines in deeper."

Darby had backed into a jumping cholla, or teddy-bear cactus. "I didn't think that I was that close," he moaned as the sharp spines began to cause some pain.

"I know," said Kevin, who had run over and was unslinging his pack. "The new spines are so light colored that it is hard to see them. It seems that the cactus jumped out and got you even before you bumped into it. If you'll just settle down for a minute, I'll pick out the spines with these pliers."

For about five minutes Kevin and the others were busy trying to make Darby a little more comfortable.

"I guess that is about all of them. At least I can't see any more," Kevin observed.

"Well, have I got news for you," Darby grimaced. "There is one spot that you haven't had a chance to work on yet. Kev, you and I have an appointment behind that large rock over there. See you later, girls."

Ramona and Marcy grinned as Kevin and Darby disappeared behind a nearby boulder to finish extracting the spines from a tender part of Darby's anatomy.

"Be sure to use some of that iodine," Ramona called after them. About ten minutes later, Kevin and a sheepish Darby rejoined the girls on the trail.

About ten o'clock Ramona called a halt, and while the hikers were drinking some water and chewing on dried fruit, Darby spotted a pile of twigs, bits of dried cactus, string, and even some rings from soft drink cans all stacked in a haphazard pile some distance on the other side of the trail.

"What's that pile of trash doing over there?" Darby asked.

"That's not trash," Marcy responded. "That's a pack rat's nest."

"What's the point of building an untidy mess that looks as though it would blow away in a good wind?" Darby wondered aloud.

"Well, can you tell where the entrance to the nest is?" questioned Kevin.

"No . . . oh, I see," Darby exclaimed. "It's hard to tell just where to go in, and this probably confuses anything that chases the rat."

"Exactly," said Marcy, "especially foxes or mountain lions. It also helps shade the burrow which is beneath the pile of junk."

Suddenly a large, brownish-black rat scrambled out of one side of the nest and hurried up the slope of a rock outcrop. Darby, unable to control himself, chased after the animal to see where it would go. When he was about halfway up the slope, Ramona shouted at him to stop. Darby, not hearing, started over the top of the ridge. Just at that moment, his foot slipped on a smooth tuft of weeds. He fell into a heap and tumbled toward the bottom of the slope.

"Are you okay?" Kevin shouted.

"Sure, a bit scratched, but O.K. What's the big commotion about?" Darby asked.

"You've got to watch where you put your hands when you're climbing, especially at this time of year," Ramona warned. "Come here. Maybe I can show you why." She picked up a long stick lying nearby and quietly moved to near the top of the ledge, where she stopped and peered cautiously over the rim. Then she beckoned quietly to the others to come silently along. When they were near enough to see, Darby barely controlled a squawk by covering his mouth with his hand.

"Holy cow, it's a rattler! And to think that I almost grabbed it!" Darby's voice was shaky.

"You don't know how close you came to using that snakebite kit you didn't want to carry," Kevin said with a grin as the group scrambled back down the rock outcrop.

When the party was once more on the trail, Darby dropped back and murmured, "Thanks a lot."

"Sure, anytime," Ramona smiled.

The hikers arrived at First Water about noon. Ramona started the primus stove and heated some soup and tea. The sandwiches quickly disappeared, and, after a brief rest, the party reassembled and started the return trip. The patches of cumulus clouds had glued themselves together, and the sky began to look as though it would rain soon. A cool breeze took away the warmth of the sun the few times it appeared from behind the clouds.

Darby was surprised to see each of the party picking up empty aluminum cans. "Why are you picking up all that junk?"

"Helps keep the trail fresh-looking, and we can get about fifteen cents a pound for the empties," Ramona told him.

"Sounds okay, especially the money part," Darby said. "I guess I can do my share. Say, how far is Larry supposed to be from here? And what did he say he was investigating? Petroglyphs? I'm not sure I know what a petroglyph is."

"They are symbols or figures that Indians have carved into rocks," Ramona said.

"Are they very old? What are they used for?"

"Some petroglyphs date back hundreds of years. Some are much more recent. The markings were probably just someone's expression of art or how they felt about an animal or someone. Some of them may have been messages to other Indians. I saw a rock once that was covered with petroglyphs. Some people claimed that it was a sort of Indian newspaper."

All this information came from Ramona.

"Didn't you say that Larry was going into a particularly rough area this time, Kevin?" asked Marcy.

"That's what he told me when he was leaving," replied Kevin with a slightly worried look. "He is a good hiker, but I sure hope that he doesn't get tangled up with some of the squatters who are looking for gold."

"Well, what's so dangerous about running into a squatter?" asked Darby.

"Usually nothing," Kevin replied. "But in the last few years everyone and his brother have been trying to find the Lost Dutchman Mine. They stake out a piece of ground, and shoot most anybody who looks as though they are about to come over the boundary of their claim. A fellow was killed in a gunfight earlier this year."

"Wow, sounds a bit hairy," Darby said.

"Well, we can't do Larry much good just sitting around worrying," said Ramona. "Let's get started back. We still have a few miles to go, and it looks as though it's going to rain."

The party trudged along in silence for the rest of the trip. They arrived at the jeep just as a heavy, soaking downpour surrounded the hikers.

"The Apache gods are unhappy," Ramona murmured, jumping into the driver's seat. Just then the lightning snapped and a loud peal of thunder followed. "They sound angry, too. I hope they calm down by tomorrow."

3
WEE-KIT-SAUR-AH

"All aboard!" shouted Ramona, revving up the engine of the Coleman family jeep. Kevin and Marcy had already loaded their packs into the four-wheel-drive vehicle and now they, along with Brig, were waiting not too patiently for Darby. It was only 7 A.M., but already the temperature was an uncomfortable 85 degrees.

"I don't see why I can't wear shorts and a sleeveless blouse," complained Marcy, unbuttoning the top button of her long-sleeved shirt.

"In the desert you try to prevent loss of body moisture," said Ramona with concern. "When we are out all day, you'll see how your perspiration will help keep you cool," she added as Darby came stumbling out of the house, his pack on his shoulder.

Kevin ran back to see that the house was locked, while Darby shoved his pack into the space behind the seats. "You're gonna be sorry you're bringing so much," said Marcy.

"We'll see who turns out to be sorry," said Darby smugly, climbing into the open jeep.

"Well, sorry or not, at least we're all here," said Ramona. Kevin climbed in and she let out the clutch. Then the car went leaping down the driveway and into the street, accompanied by loud peals of laughter.

A few minutes later as they turned onto the highway that led to the mountains, Kevin spoke. "Ramona, does it bother you? Our going into the Superstitions? What I mean is, I've heard that the mountains are sacred to the Apaches and that they don't want anyone going there."

Ramona didn't answer immediately, and at first Kevin thought that she hadn't heard him or that she was ignoring him. Marcy and Darby became silent, awaiting her reply.

At last Ramona spoke, keeping her eyes on the road ahead of her.

"There are many stories among the Indians about the Superstitions, just as there are among the white people. Different tribes have different beliefs. I have been told that Pima and Maricopa Indians who live near here completely avoid these mountains. They believe that to go near them will mean immediate death."

Marcy had stopped playing with Brig and along with the boys was giving Ramona her complete attention.

"There is even a Pima legend I heard at the Indian school," Ramona went on, "that when the Spanish came to the New World, Montezuma's tribes fled north to here. The legend says that the Aztecs live in the heart of the mountains behind a magic gateway made of stone. It is believed that someday they will come forth and reclaim the land that is theirs. The Pimas believe that anyone who stumbles into the Aztec sanctuary will be killed instantly."

Kevin was thinking of all the unexplained killings that had

taken place in these mountains and about the massacre many years ago of Peralta's people who were bringing gold from the Apache mines.

"What the Superstitions mean to us Apaches is a lot more involved," said Ramona thoughtfully. "We call the mountains Wee-Kit-Saur-Ah, which translates to something like 'Rocks Standing Up.' The mountains are the home of our Thunder Gods, and we believe that here the storms are born. We believe that our souls pass through here after death. It's kind of like what you call purgatory."

"As hot as it is today, it's more like the place down below," interrupted Darby. Marcy started to laugh, but when she saw the serious look Kevin gave her, the smile died on her lips, and Ramona continued.

"Although my people believe there are evil spirits here, we are practical about our religion. My ancestors overcame their fear of this place because it served them well as a natural fortress from the white man and from the Mexicans and from other Indian tribes, who were afraid to come up here.

"It was a good place to make raids from, and if the Apaches were being chased, it was a good hiding place.

"To keep the spirits from being angry for my ancestors' coming here, we have set aside a certain area of the mountains as sacred. Do not ask me where that area is, because I am not permitted to tell you. I can tell you that we will not be going near there on this trip, and I can never reveal to you where it is."

Everyone was silent for some time after Ramona had finished, and then Kevin spoke. "I read once that when Geronimo was being held by the soldiers in Oklahoma, he offered some of them a million dollars in gold if they would help him escape. He told them that he had it hidden in a cave in the Superstitions, but they could never find it without him."

Ramona smiled. "I have heard that story retold m times at night around the campfire. The old men say (Geronimo was a crafty man. How could he have been the great chief that he was if he hadn't been pretty smart? Some of the old men say that he knew of the white men's weakness for the yellow metal and that he knew if he could get them into the Superstitions, he could escape. The old men of my tribe say that there is no treasure."

Ramona smiled at the disappointed look on Kevin's face. "The young men of the tribe don't always believe the old men," she said. "Some of the young ones think that the old ones do not tell the truth because they are afraid that the young men will give up farming and ranching and spend all of their time hunting for gold. I believe that the gods are jealously watching it and that nothing good can come to those who try to take it."

As Ramona talked, they had been approaching the rugged Superstitions. Giant cumulus clouds formed a background for the magnificent mountains, and Kevin found it easy to believe that gods might choose such an awe-inspiring place for their home. As shadows from the clouds gave the slopes a dark and forbidding hue, Kevin thought of the line from "America the Beautiful," and he knew what the author had meant by "purple mountain majesties."

But even as large as they seemed, he found it difficult to believe they covered over a hundred thousand acres, nine times the area of Manhattan Island.

"What a place to lose a cow!" he said aloud. But he thought to himself, What a place for four kids and a dog to get lost!

As they approached the foothills, a gust of wind met them head on, and for an instant the jeep shuddered as though giant hands were trying to prevent them from entering the area. Ramona ducked her head and pushed harder on the accelerator.

"Stop! My hat! Stop!" yelled Darby just as the wind subsided and they lurched forward.

Kevin and Marcy watched fascinated as a dust devil caught the hat and lifted it momentarily. Darby looked horrified when it sailed like a Frisbee over the road and then dropped into a wash on the left side.

"It's gone for good," Marcy moaned.

"No, stop!" screamed Darby. "We can find it!"

Ramona pulled to the side of the road and stopped, and they all dashed to the spot where the hat had disappeared. While they looked up and down the arroyo, Brig bounced about, examining the cacti along the road. "I don't see it anywhere," said Kevin.

Suddenly Ramona began to laugh as she pointed toward the wash. Midway up on the other side stood a stately saguaro cactus with one arm held high and another out to the side, very much like the Statue of Liberty. Perched atop its 25-foot main trunk was Darby's red hat.

"Climb up and get it," laughed Marcy as the others joined in. But Darby had already turned and was walking dejectedly toward the jeep.

A few minutes later as they were driving along, Kevin pointed to the map and directed Ramona to turn off and follow a dry wash.

"I think it might be a good idea to find a shady spot most anywhere along here," said Kevin.

The clouds had begun to move out and the sun beat down from high overhead. Ramona drove several hundred feet before letting up on the accelerator. Spotting a paloverde tree that provided a small amount of shade, she turned the wheel and headed toward it. Immediately the jeep slowed and then stopped, its wheels buried deep in the sand.

"I blew it!" moaned Ramona.

"Don't gun it," warned Kevin. "We'll only get stuck

deeper. We'll just leave it here for now. At least no one else can steal it. Larry'll know how to get it out."

After Ramona had turned off the ignition, her face took on a look of deep concern which only Kevin noticed as he followed her gaze toward the sky. Marcy and Darby busied themselves unloading the gear, eager to have a snack.

"Hey, you two, quit gawking and help unload!" Marcy shouted. And then she saw. High in the sky six black buzzards were circling lower and lower toward them.

4

APACHE REVENGE

"I sure hate to leave the jeep out in the open. I had a safe spot already picked out for it at the Dons' camp," Ramona murmured as she gave a last look at the machine with its wheels locked in the sand. "I guess there isn't much of a chance to rock it out, so we might as well leave it here. O.K., everybody help get the tarp over the top."

In just a few minutes the jeep was snug under a canvas cover, everyone in the party had his pack on his back, and all were ready to start hiking. This time, Darby's pack was trail ready. "It looks as though you could hike ten miles and not lose your bedroll," Kevin joked.

"Yeah, and it feels snugger and much better than yesterday," Darby replied. "Sure wish I had my hat though. It is getting pretty warm."

Ramona set a rather rapid pace along the road that sloped up into the mountains. As they moved along, they passed the buzzards flapping noisily about a dead cow.

"Yech," grunted Darby, "look how bloated it is."

"It sure doesn't take long in this heat," Kevin grimaced,

wrinkling his nose. "It must have died a couple of days ago by stumbling into that rabbit hole and breaking its neck. It looks as though some coyotes have already chewed on it, and now these buzzards. I think it was a stray from the Quarter Circle U Ranch."

"But isn't that some distance from here?" Ramona asked.

"I know, but there is no doubt about the brand on the flank. I remember it from the time I visited Danny earlier this spring when they were branding at the ranch."

With a last distasteful look, the party passed by and soon found itself moving into Peralta Canyon. About half a mile farther along, the light-duty road ended, and only a footpath remained.

"Time out for a pack check," Ramona called out. "Go easy on the water, Darby. We won't find any more until we get to some springs up the trail a few miles. You'll have to learn to ration how much you drink."

A short time later the hikers started out again. The last traces of the spring rains were disappearing from the canyons, and the first signs of the parched look of summer could be seen in the brown, shriveled look of the once-green stems of the bluebonnet and desert poppy. Each hiker's head was bent so that his eyes could more easily warn of the almost-hidden fishhook cactus, which grew close to the ground and of the loose rock that could cause a turned ankle or a nasty spill. Their breath came in a deep, steady rhythm that didn't permit singing or joking. For Darby, at least, hiking had become a chore.

After a while the trail again led uphill, and soon the hikers were skirting along the side of Fremont's Saddle, so called because of the two rock pinnacles with a low sloping area between. On top of one horn of the saddle, Ramona brought the puffing party to a halt and announced, "This looks like a good place for lunch. We have a swell view, especially of part of the trail we'll be traveling this afternoon."

Packs were dropped along the path, and Marcy and Kevin propped themselves against the shady side of a large rock. Their freckled faces were rosy and shiny from the sweat of their climbing, but they looked ready to go on. Darby, although he said nothing, showed the strains of hiking more than the others. He spread-eagled himself facedown on a sandy spot and rested his head on his arm.

Kevin glanced over and said with a grin, "It looks as though your get-up-and-go has got up and went." Darby returned Kevin's smile with a lift of his eyebrows and a short grunt. Brigadoon was the only perky one in the group. He perched himself on a small rock, wagging his black plume of a tail, and peered from one person to another as though he wanted everyone to know that he was ready to take off again at any time. Kevin gave him some water in a small plastic bowl that doubled as a feeding dish at mealtime.

"Darby, would you like to know the story of Massacre Canyon, which is not far from here?" Ramona asked.

"Didn't know there was a story," came Darby's muffled response. "If you can talk, I can listen." Darby soon forgot how hot and tired he was as Marcy, Kevin, and Ramona unfolded the tale of the Don Miguel Peralta mining party as they searched for gold in the Superstition Mountains.

It was the spring of 1847. The sun shone down warmly on Don Miguel Peralta as he headed south to his home in Sonora, Mexico. Behind Don Miguel, and following each other at rather wide intervals, were members of Peralta's party, each mounted on a horse and leading a small train of three mules heavily loaded with leather saddlebags packed with high-grade gold ore. The heat of midmorning and the slow clip-clopping of the horses' feet lulled Don Miguel into daydreaming about the yellow treasure.

The gold had been almost fantastically easy to come by.

Veins of the yellow mineral seemed to pop up almost everywhere. Don Miguel decided that he had indeed found one of the Seven Cities of Cibola that the Franciscan missionary Marcos de Niza had told about almost one hundred and fifty years before. Well, no matter about the history of the gold, it was a heaven-sent blessing at this time. The Peralta family silver mines in Sonora were not producing much, and it was rumored that soon Mexico would sign a treaty with the United States and the gold-mining country would be off limits to Mexican miners.

Up ahead, Don Miguel noticed that the trail was coming out of the mountains and giving way to flat desert country. Peralta felt much more at ease when he saw that the last of the mules was out of the mountains and headed south. He had an edgy feeling, in the hills, that someone was watching as his party stripped bag after bag of ore from the rich veins of gold. True, there had been that unpleasant incident when one of his men had become drunk and had shot one of the Apache warriors. Peralta's man had said that it was self-defense, that he thought the Indian was going to stab him with a knife. Even so, it was an unfortunate incident, and there was much talk between Don Miguel and the Apache chief, Cochise, before an uneasy peace returned to the mining operations.

The Peralta party had returned to the mountains the following year and found the mining even more rewarding. Don Miguel was overjoyed when the miners discovered the mother lode that supplied all of the veins, a lode so rich that gold nuggets fell out of the pink quartz when it was struck with a hammer. The eighteen smaller mines and this incredibly rich mother lode proved to be a lavish bonanza, supplying enough income for the Peralta family to return to Spain in splendor.

Another incident had occurred on this trip. During an

especially wild drinking party, the Indians were treated in a rough manner. The next morning one of the miners was found spitted like a roast across the campfire with his scalp hacked away. It was this last act that led Don Miguel to believe that he ought to get out before the saddlebags were full. Perhaps by next year the Indian tempers would subside a bit. Now only an hour's ride separated his party from the safety of the open desert.

At that moment a group of Apaches, scattered on both sides of the trail and above the Peralta party, rose silently from behind the rocks and let loose a storm of arrows. There was immediate panic among the Spaniards. Peralta quickly urged his men forward because there was little hope of fighting successfully from the canyon floor. But Cochise and his party had blocked the path ahead with brush and loose rocks. Peralta shouted to his men to abandon their packtrains and to escape as best they could. The Spanish rifles were of little help against an enemy that was almost invisible and constantly on the move. In a short time the Apache noose closed more tightly. Within an hour all in the Peralta party had been slaughtered, packtrains had been rounded up, and the Indians had prepared a feast. The mules, considered a tasty treat, were cooked by the women. Meanwhile, the men were busy scattering the remains of the stolen gold. Several warriors made sure that the mines were thoroughly covered so that no future invaders could discover them. The feast lasted several days until finally the Apaches felt that their gods could again be happy and dwell in peace, undisturbed by white men seeking to rob them of their riches.

As the story of the Peralta massacre came to a close, Ramona noticed that a compact, oddly shaped cloud had appeared and covered the face of the sun. It was the only cloud in the sky, and to the hikers it looked like a huge bank of mountain ramparts, not unlike the Superstition Mountains themselves. Ramona struggled back into her pack, all the while urging the others to do the same. She took one final look at the strange cloud and wondered aloud, "We are near the sacred resting place of my people's gods. Perhaps they have heard us and want us to know that they still guard this area against all unfriendly invaders."

5

A CAVE AND SOME COBS

With Ramona again in the lead, the party started along the trail, following the contour of Fremont's Saddle. For a change, the walking was on level ground and everyone, including Brigadoon and Darby, scooted along at a fairly brisk pace. After a while the trail swung down to a lower level and turned sharply to the left. As the group rounded the corner, they were greeted with an abrupt change of scenery. The usual dry countryside with its cacti and mesquite disappeared, and a small oasislike area greeted the hikers. Two sycamore trees in full leaf towered overhead and gave inviting shade to a small pool of water underneath. The pool was fed by a spring from which only a small trickle of moisture slowly dripped over moss-covered rocks and into a basin that had formed in a broad flat rock. The slender sharp leaves of a clump of bear grass swayed gently in the breeze. Several stalks of orange-red Indian paintbrush added a splash of color.

Darby rushed over to plunge his face into the pool, only to be brought up short by Ramona. "Easy, Darby—let's fill our canteens first and then wait until the basin fills up again."

Darby smiled a bit sheepishly and reminded himself, "I still have some water in my canteen."

In addition to their canteens, each hiker had in his pack a quart plastic flask, which was filled from the basin. The process took an hour or so, but no one seemed to mind. Brigadoon snuffled happily in the wet moss and rolled about in the small clumps of grass before finally curling up in the shade of a tree for a short nap.

While they waited for the rock basin to fill, Kevin, Marcy, and Darby watched Ramona move to a bunch of long, slender, saw-toothed leaves, and carefully cut one free from its base near the ground. By trimming the top and smoothing out the bottom edges, Ramona was able to make a spoon to ladle water from the basin.

"Great idea," exclaimed Kevin as he dug into his shirt pocket and produced his knife. He cut a leaf spoon for each of the others, and soon they were busy slurping up the water as fast as the basin filled.

"We'll have to make the water in our plastic bottles do for the next day and a half," Ramona warned. "There are no other springs until we get to Williams Camp. We ought to make out O.K. if we conserve our supply. Just don't drink every time you feel like it. And chew some gum. It helps keep your mouth moist."

"How much farther up the trail will we hike today?" Darby asked. He didn't seem particularly tired. The rest period had perked up his body as well as his mind, and he seemed to be settling into the role of a seasoned hiker.

"Well, not too much farther." A thoughtful frown wrinkled Ramona's forehead. "We have about an hour and a half until we come to Geronimo's cave. I think you'll like staying there for the night."

Each hiker got out a handkerchief, dipped it in the pool,

draped the wet cloth over his head and headed along the trail. About three o'clock in the afternoon, Ramona led the group down a wide, dry wash where a few scraggly cottonwood trees fought a losing battle against the heat and too little water. The walking was fairly easy. At one place the wash jutted out to the right and then suddenly back to the left behind a stunted sycamore tree. Ahead loomed the canyon wall. Ramona led the party out of the wash, up to the foot of the canyon, and pointed upward. "That's where we'll be sleeping tonight."

All eyes followed the direction of her hand, and the hikers gaped as they saw a cave opening that pierced the side of the canyon wall. The cave had been carved out by water when flash floods roared down the wash. It seemed as though a giant hand had scooped out a place in the rock. Dirt and boulders, piled up by floods, provided an easy path up to the entrance, where a low stone wall gave shelter from animals and the wind.

Darby and Kevin needed no urging to start scrambling up the path to the entrance and over the wall into the cave's cool interior. They stood and watched while the girls followed at a more leisurely pace.

"Absolutely fantastic," Darby murmured as he looked around. "How long have you known about this place, Ramona?"

"I passed by here about a year ago with my brother," Ramona replied. "We didn't stop then, and I've always wanted to stay overnight. Let's have a look around."

Everyone got out his flashlight and moved through a small door at the rear of the wall that divided the cave into two main parts. Marcy commented that the wall must have been made by hand, for the rocks were smooth and rounded and were held together by a rough mortar which was still firm. The sides and top of the door were made of small tree limbs that showed where the branches had been snapped off by some Indian carpenter long ago.

The extra room was small with a low ceiling and no opening to the outside. The flashlight beams bouncing from the walls gave the place an eerie look and emphasized the dustiness of the air. Darby's light played over the rear wall and then suddenly stopped to reveal a small hole about three feet above the floor.

"Hey, look," Darby whispered. "A storage place for something. Let's get a closer look."

Everyone scrambled over to the hole, and while Marcy shone a light into the area, Darby poked about with a stick. Nothing rattled, hissed, or sprang at him, so he gingerly put his arm in and after a moment shouted, "I've found something! I've found something!"

"Well, don't just stand there shouting, let the rest of us see," Kevin said impatiently.

Slowly, Darby pulled out an earthen pot with several pieces chipped from the rim. It was a gracefully shaped thing, made of tan mud that had been baked in the sun. "There's something inside. Let's dump the stuff on the floor."

Everyone's light joined to form a wavering circle into which Darby poured six tiny corncobs, each about three inches long.

"Well, I'll be doggoned," whispered Kevin. "I wonder where these came from?"

"I think I know," Ramona said thoughtfully. "My grandfather told me that four or five hundred years ago some small bands of Indians settled near the streams and lived where they could grow food. This miniature corn was one thing they ate, along with squash and probably beans. They lived here until a long dry spell made it impossible to grow anything."

"But they are so tiny," Marcy said.

"True, but the Indians of those days hadn't heard of hybrid corn with ears a foot long," Ramona explained. "I imagine that they were glad to get an ear this size."

Darby had remained silent up to now, but his face was thoughtful and showed wonderment. "I just can't believe it! I am holding some food that was stored five hundred years ago in an Indian's pantry. It's enough to blow your mind."

Although it was still light enough for them to see to gather wood, the setting sun cast long shadows as the weary hikers began to plan their evening meal. Even Darby, who had not missed a chance all day to voice his complaints, busily gathered skeletons of dead cholla cactus for the fire. The others joined him in the search for any kind of firewood, all of them knowing that the sooner they got the fire going, the sooner they would eat. Ramona looked for mesquite as the smell of its burning reminded her of cookouts during cattle drives when she was younger. The others forgot their weariness as they fanned out from the campsite.

"Look what I found!" exclaimed Marcy, who had been scouting in a small side canyon, out of the others' sight. She came into the campground, dragging behind her a log about four feet in length. It was charred on one end and had obviously been brought in by other campers, since there were no trees of any size near their camping spot. "This'll burn all night, and there's another just like it," Marcy added.

"Way to go," congratulated Kevin.

"Good girl," Ramona chimed in, smiling her approval.

"I'll get the other one," said Marcy proudly and skipped off in the direction from which she had come.

As Kevin knelt to begin laying the fire and Darby brought in a small load of various size sticks, Ramona began to check their food supply.

"Hey, Ramona," asked Kevin, "you wanna rub two sticks together and get this fire going?"

Ramona laughed. "Sure, paleface," she said, "you gotta couple of matches?"

Kevin's answering laugh was interrupted by a loud, frightened scream, unmistakably Marcy's. Dropping what they were doing, Ramona, Kevin, and Darby all ran toward the direction from which the scream had come. But only a few feet from the campsite, they met up with the wide-eyed ten-year-old. Breathlessly she ran to Kevin, pulled on his arm, and implored, "Don't go up there!" She pointed toward the small canyon where she had been gathering wood.

Ramona put her arms about Marcy's shoulders. "Calm down! Calm down! What's wrong? Tell us what's wrong. You're okay now. Did you see a snake or something?" she asked.

"N-n-n-no," Marcy sputtered. "N-n-not a snake! A m-m-man!"

"You mean a dead man?" asked Darby, always ready to add mystery to any event.

"No, no," said Marcy, becoming calmer, yet exasperated by his question. She wiped the perspiration from her face, spreading black charcoal from the log across her forehead. The dark grime covered her freckles and gave her an even more wide-eyed appearance. Brig, who had been doing his own exploring, joined the group and began barking and growling excitedly.

"It's a real live man," said Marcy. "He's got a burro and a beard and . . . and . . . and . . ." She stopped, momentarily unable to speak. "And there he is now," she shrieked, pointing up the canyon.

6

THE LOST DUTCHMAN?

Kevin, Ramona, and Darby turned to look. Brig began to bark uncontrollably. Emerging from behind a tall creosote bush, a stocky, red-faced man made his way toward them, leading a gray, overloaded donkey. He made no sign of greeting, but upon seeing them, he stopped and, pulling a red bandana handkerchief from his hip pocket, wiped his sunburned face. Kevin bent to pick up a heavy stick.

Ramona began to lead Marcy back toward the campsite, but the two boys remained, watching the approaching stranger. Brig advanced toward the visitor, uttering deep growls. Suddenly he yelped, stopped growling, and scurried back to stand beside the boys.

Squinting into the setting sun, the boys momentarily lost sight of the bearded man and his donkey. The mountain seemed to have swallowed him.

"Hey, he's gone," Darby said incredulously.

Kevin was just about to agree when he heard the sound of the donkey's hooves and, shading his eyes, was able to see the figures. Darby squatted to the ground and tried to appear casual as he picked up a rock. Kevin gripped his club more tightly. The stranger approached to within fifteen feet of the boys. Then he stopped and carefully studied them. Seemingly relieved to see that they were boys rather than men, he smiled and spoke with a thick accent.

"Vell! Vhat are you two boys doing out here in the middle of novhere?" His smile was friendly, and although Kevin remained wary, Darby dropped his guard.

"We came up here to meet Kevin's brother, Larry. Larry's looking for Indian writing. Kevin here's my cousin," said Darby smiling. "My name's Darby Driscoll."

The stranger smiled back. "Just call me Jake," he said.

Kevin reached out to shake Jake's hand, but the man turned and began to adjust his pack. "I hope I didn't scare the little girl," he said. "I was coming down the canyon and there she was."

"She's okay," said Darby. "You just kind of surprised her, I guess."

"Are you a prospector?" asked Kevin, noting the shovel and pans sticking out of the pack on the burro.

"This is rough country for a little girl to be in," said Jake, avoiding Kevin's question. "Strange things have been known to happen to people up here."

"We know that," replied Darby. "But we're well prepared. We've got plenty of food and water, and we've got a map to show us where to find Larry."

Kevin gave Darby a disapproving look, but he was not to be stopped. "Our jeep is stuck in the sand somewhere back there," said Darby, pointing. "But ole Larry'll know how to get it out. We're all right. Matter of fact, we're just getting ready to eat right now. Care to join us?"

Jake stopped fiddling with his pack and turned to face the boys, smiling broadly. "Vell," he grinned, "that's vhat I call very kind of you. Old Jake could sure use a good meal."

"Just follow us," said Darby. "Come on, Kev, we'd better go help the girls."

Ramona had kept Marcy busy while the boys had been talking to Jake. She knew that Marcy was a brave girl, but the shock of seeing another human being out in the vast wilderness was enough to frighten even a grown-up. And the man known as Jake had appeared so suddenly that Marcy was startled. Working with Ramona, she had regained her calm and was busily opening a can of pork and beans as Ramona coaxed the fire to life.

"What do you suppose that old man is doing out here?" asked Marcy.

"I can't say for sure," answered Ramona. "But these mountains are full of foolish men who think that they can find the gold of the Apaches. He's probably just another one of the men who believe all the stories that they hear in bars on skid row in Phoenix. He probably gave some old wino five dollars for a map that he thinks will lead him to the gold. Personally, I'd feel better if he just kept moving along. The sun gets to some of these men and they do crazy things."

At that moment, Darby, Kevin, and Jake came up. As Kevin began gathering some of the scattered gear, Darby announced, "Put on an extra can of beans, girls. We're having a guest for dinner."

Ramona looked at Kevin, who nodded to show that it was all right, although he didn't seem happy about having the older man around. Jake tied his burro to a low bush and removed a leather pouch from one of the saddlebags. Placing the pouch in his pocket, he seated himself on a rock and eyed the food hungrily.

Darby was strangely elated at having Jake in camp, and while the others busied themselves with the meal, he devoted his attention to the old prospector. Jake answered each question Darby asked, but he offered no additional information about himself.

"How long have you been out here?" asked Darby.

"One month," said Jake.

"Have you seen many people?"

"No," answered Jake.

"What's your last name?"

Pretending not to have heard the question, Jake rose and walked to his burro. "I think I'll unload Julia and tie her over here a vays," he said, pointing to a rock about twenty yards from the campsite. He took the rope halter and began walking with the burro down the slope away from the camp.

As soon as Jake was out of earshot, Darby loudly whispered, "Kevin!" and began motioning to his cousin to come over to where he was standing.

At first Kevin ignored him, but as Darby became more insistent, Kevin stopped what he was doing and asked, "What do you want? I have to get this stuff unpacked before it gets dark."

"Hurry," whispered Darby. "I have to tell you something before he gets back."

Kevin shrugged and walked over. Together the boys strolled to the small side canyon.

"Okay, be quick," urged Kevin. "I don't want to leave the girls alone too long."

"All right then. Listen carefully," whispered Darby. He hesitated. "I know you're gonna think I'm crazy," he apologized, "but do you know who Jake really is?"

"Yeah," replied Kevin. "He's some old man who's been out in the sun too long."

"No," sputtered Darby. "Be serious and think a minute. What's Jake a nickname for?"

"Jake? Jacob, I suppose," answered Kevin.

"And what nationality would you say he is?" asked Darby.

"German or Dutch, I guess."

"Okay, doesn't that tell you something?"

For a moment Kevin stood with a blank look on his face. Gradually a smile formed on his lips. Then the smile became a broad grin, and finally Kevin broke into peals of raucous laughter.

"Be quiet," warned Darby. "He's gonna hear you."

"I hope he does," laughed Kevin. "He'll probably think you're as funny as I do." Kevin guffawed again, and then, trying to control himself, he asked, "Do you really think our friend Jake is Jacob Walz or Waltz or whatever? Do you think he's the Dutchman who found the mine here years ago?"

"Why not?" asked Darby.

"Well, first of all, Jacob Walz died in Phoenix in the 1890's and he was over eighty years old then."

"Yeah," replied Darby. "And who was the woman who was taking care of him at that time, if you know so much?"

"Her name was Julia Thomas," countered Kevin.

"Right," said Darby. "And what did Jake call his donkey just now? 'Julia!' Right?"

"Darby, I think the sun has gotten to you, too. Who do you think we've been talking to—a ghost? For a mirage, he sure has a lot of human qualities. Did you see him looking at that food and licking his chops? Come on. Let's get back before he eats it all." Kevin started to walk away.

"Okay," said Darby. "But I still think that Jake and the Dutchman are the same person. I can't explain it, but I'll bet if we follow him, he'll lead us to the mine."

"Come on. Let's eat," said Kevin.

"Just one more thing." Darby grabbed his cousin's arm. "Did you notice how Brig acted? He was really afraid. He usually isn't scared of man or beast, but he wouldn't have anything to do with Jake. You can believe what you want, but

I think Jake is the Dutchman, or at least he has something to do with him."

Kevin turned and walked back toward the campsite. He wanted to think that Darby was just letting his imagination run wild, but he couldn't shake the feeling that maybe part of what his cousin was saying had a ring of truth to it.

7

JAKE DISAPPEARS

It was nearly dark by the time they had eaten and had stored their utensils. The last glow of the sunset formed a crimson backdrop to the range of mountains far to the east. A deep silence had fallen over the Superstitions, broken only by the occasional conversation of the four young people or by the distant hoot of a desert owl.

Old Jake, who had filled and emptied his plate twice, sat by himself, picking his teeth with a sliver he had whittled from a piece of desert sage. As he rested, he watched each of the young people intently as they gathered their mess kits and washed them by rubbing them with sand. Ramona looked with approval as Marcy tossed each scrap of paper into the campfire and gathered the empty cans to put into her pack.

"Now's the time to put your log on, Marcy," said Kevin as he piled more rocks around the fire.

Deciding that it was time for bed, Brig climbed the rocks to the cave. After smelling each sleeping bag, he chose Darby's, turned three small circles, and lay down. Heaving a long sigh, he closed his eyes and began to dream of chasing jackrabbits.

"Where shall we store the food?" asked Marcy, turning to her brother.

"Well, let's see," answered Kevin, surveying the area and pretending not to be aware of Jake. "I guess we can just put it up in the cave."

"May I make a suggestion?" asked Jake, rising to his feet. "You know there are some coyotes and mountain lions up here. They may come prowling around looking for food during the night. If I were you, I'd hang your food up somewhere out of their reach."

"Where do you suggest?" asked Darby agreeably.

"What about up in that tree?" Jake pointed down the trail. "The coyotes can't get at the food there, and it's not strong enough to support the weight of a mountain lion. It'll be safe there."

"Sounds great to me," agreed Darby, looking to Kevin for approval. "That way those animals won't come prowling around the cave."

Kevin didn't like the idea because Jake had suggested it. He still didn't trust Jake. But after thinking about it, he remembered that Jake had said he had been in the Superstitions for about a month. The old boy should know what he's doing, Kevin thought.

Darby and Kevin picked up the backpacks containing the food and carried them down to the tree. In the waning light they hung them as high as they could and then returned to camp.

Suddenly it was dark, and although it was still quite warm, the fire was a welcome sight in the vast darkness that surrounded them.

Ramona passed around a bag of caramels as the group gathered near the campfire. They sat in silence, looking up at the fireworks display that was provided by the millions of stars in the Arizona sky.

Even Darby remained strangely quiet, but his fidgeting revealed that his mind was wrestling with some deep problem. When he finally spoke, his voice quavered, and he had to stop and begin again.

"Jake," he began, "did you . . . I mean have you . . . I guess I mean have you ever heard of Jacob Walz?"

A coyote howled in the distance as Jake spoke. "I am Jacob Walz," he answered calmly.

Kevin jumped to his feet, and Marcy moved closer to Ramona. Darby sat in wide-eyed wonder, a strange, knowing smile on his face.

"Do you mean you're the Dutchman of the Lost Dutchman Mine?" he asked, ready to believe anything.

Jake chuckled dryly. "No," he said. "I am the grandson of Jacob Walz, who discovered what is called the Lost Dutchman Mine. Actually, my grandfather was German rather than Dutch."

"If he was your grandfather," asked Kevin, "why do you have an accent? After all, weren't you born in this country?"

Jake was annoyed. *"Nein,"* he snapped. "Like my grandfather and father, I was born in Germany. My grandfather wanted to get rich quickly, and when he heard of the gold strikes in America, he hurried to Arizona to work in the mines and to make his fortune.

"Somewhere," said Jake thoughtfully, "maybe at the Vulture Mine, my grandfather met an Apache girl named Ken-tee. I do not know all of the story, but for some reason she led him here, to the Superstitions, and showed him where he could find the Apache gold. On their first trip from the mountains, they carried out thousands of dollars in gold ore."

Ramona had heard of Ken-tee. The Apaches had watched as Ken-tee and Walz returned from the home of the Thunder

Gods. They knew that she had done a terrible thing by taking a white man to the sacred place, and they knew that she must not be allowed to tell anyone else. They had raided the place where Ken-tee was staying and had kidnapped her. White neighbors had chased after the Apaches and had killed some of them. But before the white men could reach Ken-tee, the Apaches had cut out her tongue to keep her silent. She had died soon after that, but Jacob had learned the secret of the Apache treasure.

Darby rose and added another log to the fire. Marcy yawned, stood up, and stretched. She did not want to miss any part of the story, even if she wasn't sure she believed the strange, bearded man.

Jake continued his story. "After that, my grandfather became a lonely, suspicious man. He knew that people were trying to find out from him about the location of the mine. He carried a rifle and a pistol wherever he went. Always people were following him to try to find the mine. They tried in every way—threats, friendship, money—to learn the secret, but he would not tell them. When he built his house in Phoenix, it was like a fort. The walls were four feet thick, and there was only one door. He became distrustful of everyone.

"For many years he went to the mine only when he needed money. He went only at night, and he used many tricks to be sure that nobody was following him. It is said that when my grandfather died, he left a map showing how to find the lost mine. So far, no one has found the true map or the mine."

"And now you have come to try to steal the Apache gold," said Ramona, unable to control her anger.

"Have no fear about your sacred ground, my red-skinned friend," answered Jake gently. "I am here as a visitor. In Germany, I am a wealthy man. I came here only to see the place where my grandfather lived. I have visited long enough and soon I will be returning to Germany. I thank you very much for your hospitality this evening."

Shortly after finishing his story, Jake bid them all a short good-night and curled up in a blanket in the shadows away from the fire. It wasn't long until all of the young people were zipped up in their sleeping bags. The desert hollow had cooled quickly in the night air, and everyone settled in for a sound sleep.

Sometime during the night Darby was awakened by Brig's low growl.

"What's wrong, boy?" asked Darby, sitting up in his sleeping bag and listening. He reached out and grabbed Brig's collar and pulled him over. "Did you hear a coyote or something?"

Brig growled once more and lay down, his chin resting on Darby's leg.

"That's a good boy," said Darby, patting him on the head. "Go to sleep."

Ramona was the first to awaken in the morning. She looked at the others, still sleeping, and decided not to awaken them. Using a premoistened towel, she washed her face. With a bunch of dry desert grass she rekindled the coals of the fire. Then she slowly added larger and larger sticks until she had a steady blaze for the morning's meal.

Taking a spoon and the largest of the pans from among the supplies, Ramona walked quietly back to the sleeping trio. Only Brig was awake. He pricked up his ears and turned his head from side to side, trying to understand what she was about to do.

BANG! BANG! Bang! Bang! Bang! went the sound of the spoon on the pan as Ramona began to dance around her startled friends, chanting in her native Apache language and laughing with great glee. Adding to the din, Brig began to bark loudly.

The sleepers' eyes popped open, and startled looks changed to grumpy frowns. But frowns were quickly replaced by smiles at the sight of Ramona and her dancing. Kevin was the first to get in line behind her. Marcy soon joined them, and the three pulled a more reluctant Darby from the cocoon of his sleeping bag. Uncertainly Darby joined them, and the dancing continued for a few more seconds. Then they all fell laughing in a happy heap on their sleeping bags.

"What's for breakfast?" asked Marcy. "I'm starved."

"Well," replied Ramona, trying to run a comb through Marcy's tousled hair, "if these lazy lugs will get their boots on and go get the food out of the tree, we'll have a look. The fire is ready and we can eat anytime."

This statement was all the boys needed. They headed toward the paloverde where they had left the food.

As they neared the tree, Darby looked around. "I wonder where my Dutchman is?" he asked, seeing that Jake was not in the spot he had picked for his campground. He turned to Kevin for an answer and saw the worried look in his cousin's brown eyes.

"We're in trouble, Darb," said Kevin, staring at the tree. "Old Jake has high-graded us and taken the food. We're in real trouble!"

"Oh, no," moaned Darby, his voice rising. "So that's what Brig was growling about. Well, at least he left our other packs and the things we had in the cave. What are we going to do now, Kevin?"

"First of all, let's stay calm and not alarm the girls. Let's check to make sure that he's really gone." Kevin climbed up on a rock and surveyed the surrounding area. "He's gone, all right," he said finally.

Darby had been checking the ground where the German had been sleeping. He knelt for a moment and then stood up, staring wide-eyed at an object in his hand.

"Kevin, come quick!" he screamed. "Look what he left. A gold nugget!"

Kevin jumped from the rock and rushed over to Darby. After examining the object, he said, "I think that's a gold nugget, all right, but we're not going to be able to eat or drink it in the next two days. I'm sorry I didn't trust you, Darby. I hung some of our water supply over here so you wouldn't get too tempted during the night. He's taken that, too."

8

LOOK BEFORE YOU LEAP!

What had started out to be a cheerful day full of new adventure suddenly took on a somber and downhearted mood.

"Man, oh man, am I hungry," grumbled Kevin.

"And thinking about not having anything to eat makes me even hungrier," Darby added. "Well, we are not really down-and-out. I left my canteen in the cave along with Kevin's, and both of them were almost full. I also have six beef jerky sticks and some chewing gum in my bedroll. I'll be glad to share." The last remark was offered with pride, and the others realized that Darby wouldn't have acted so generously just a few days ago.

The others volunteered what little food they could find in their jackets and what had been left around the campfire from the night before. A final check showed that, in addition to Darby's contributions, the entire grocery supply consisted of a small can each of pork and beans and one of vienna sausages, a dozen pieces of candy, and some powdered orange drink.

"A lot of good orange drink does if we don't have water to mix with it. I'm so mad I could spit!" stormed Marcy.

"Better not," joked Kevin. "You may need all the spit you can get before we get out of this mess."

"Which leads us to the next thing," said Ramona in her quiet way. "We've got to make some decision about our plans. Do we go on, or do we go back?"

"Do we really have much of a choice?" Darby asked. "It's a day's hike back to our starting place. How far is it if we decide to go ahead as we had originally planned, Ramona?"

"It would take us about the same length of time, either way, although the hiking is a little tougher in some spots from here on," Ramona answered.

"Aren't we forgetting that the jeep is stuck? We'd have to hike five or six miles farther just to get to the highway before we could even start hitchhiking back to Apache Junction," Kevin told the others. "If we're worried about food, we can probably get some at the cowboy line shack at Williams Camp. We can replace what we take later."

"Well, I suspect that we'd make it to the camp without too much trouble, but we'd have to agree to be very careful about how we rationed food and water," Ramona replied with a slight frown. "One thing we can't control worries me."

"I'll bet I know what it is," said Marcy. "It's the dirty Dutchman or German, or whatever he is. Why didn't he pick on someone his own size? And why did he have to take all of our food and the extra water bottles? He didn't look skinny enough to be starving."

Ramona spoke aloud, but almost as though she were talking to herself. "I can't be sure, but I don't believe all that stuff he said about just looking around to see where his grandfather had traveled. I'll bet that he has been searching for the lost gold mine himself. He imagined that we might stumble onto the mine before he did, and by taking our food, he was discouraging us before we got too close."

"I'd swap him the mine for our breakfast anytime now," Darby said, trying to ignore the rumbling in his stomach. "However, I'll be danged if I want to retreat after coming this far. Now that we know we have an enemy, we can keep our eyes peeled for him."

"Do you reckon we'll come across him again?" Marcy asked, drawing her sweater closer around her in spite of the fact that the morning was getting quite warm. "We may not be so lucky the next time. But I'll go along with Darby. I'd rather stick it out than backtrack."

There was almost immediate agreement from Kevin and Ramona that the group should continue with the original plan. Ramona suggested that they collect some water before they started out, and after a skimpy breakfast, Darby and Ramona formed one work party, and Kevin and Marcy another. They agreed that if they built two solar stills, they could get enough water to start their trip later in the day.

They chose a sunny spot in the wash near one bank where the weed growth showed that some water was near the surface of the ground. Each took his turn digging with canteen cups, tree branches, and hands until they had hollowed out a pit about forty inches across and about two feet deep. The insides sloped downward and flattened out to form a shelf near the bottom. In the center of the bottom was a small hole big enough to hold a canteen cup.

The boys went scouting along the wash for prickly-pear cacti, and each cut as many pads as he could drag back. This was the most dangerous part of the job, for the spines on the cacti made it impossible to carry many pads at one time. Finally, Darby stripped off his shirt and used it for a basket. Each pad was chopped in small pieces and placed on the shelf at the bottom of the pit. Ramona and Kevin carefully placed a poncho over the hole with enough slack in the middle so that the stone they put there sank the poncho into a point just over the cup. Finally, they sealed the poncho carefully around the edges with dirt.

"I don't see just how this thing is going to get us any water," Darby grumbled as he wiped the sweat out of his eyes with a dirty forearm.

Kevin stopped work and leaned back on one leg. "Well, the sunlight heats the inside of the pit and some of the water stored in the cacti evaporates. The tiny water drops then hit the poncho and form larger drops, which finally run down into the cup. Neat, huh?"

"Yeah, neat all right, but will it work?"

"Wait and see."

Which is just what everyone did for the remainder of the morning. The water-collecting process was a slow one, but after the cactus stems had been changed several times, two canteens had been filled with water that was fit to drink, though it was a bit sandy and tasted a little like cactus pulp. There was even enough left over for everyone to have about a quarter of a cup while they packed and started up the wash. Before they moved out, Ramona got them together and explained that she wanted to take another trail to try to make up for the time they had lost in the morning. It would be a first time over the new route for her, but it seemed no harder than the one they had originally planned to take, and it was lot shorter. She got no argument from the others, and soon the hikers were strung out along the trail, working their way to the top of a nearby plateau, and then up slopes that led slowly but surely higher.

About three in the afternoon everyone gladly agreed to take a brief siesta under the scanty shade of a paloverde tree. They shared a beef jerky stick and each had a piece of candy, washed down with a few swallows of the water from the solar still.

Ramona sat up suddenly, snapped her fingers, and exclaimed, "What is the matter with me? Why haven't I thought of it before?"

"Thought of what?" Marcy asked.

"Of the prickly-pear fruit. We've been passing them all the way up the slope."

"Do you mean that we've been missing out on something to eat?" Darby inquired in a somewhat angry tone.

"Well, they are not exactly a double cheeseburger with the trimmings, but they can help quench our thirst. Come on, I'll show you. Kevin, Darby . . . lend me your pocketknives."

Soon Ramona was spearing one of the bright red fruits perched atop each pad. With the second knife, she peeled away the skin, which was polka-dotted here and there with tufts of bristles. The scarlet fruit inside was greeted with a grateful "ummm" as Darby chewed on the piece Ramona had given him.

"It is juicy and tastes a little like pomegranate," he said. "There are lots of seeds, though."

"Stop grumbling and eat," Kevin came back. "There are plenty more where that came from."

"Be sure not to eat any without skinning them first," Ramona warned. "Those little bristles look harmless enough, but they can stick in your lips and tongue. You have to scrape them free once they get under your skin."

When they had eaten their fill, the group started up the slope, which was becoming steeper. At the top they could see a row of rocks rising out of the ground. About half an hour later they scrambled over the last rise in the ground and came to an abrupt halt. The valley floor suddenly spread out before them. As they looked around, it became clear to all, especially Ramona, that they were atop a cliff that dropped straight down for seventy-five feet to a small meadow below.

On each side, as far as they could see, stretched the exposed top of a rocky ridge. Kevin got down on his belly and wriggled as close as he could to the edge. "The rocks are strange-looking," he said. "They have split and worn away into long blocks. They look like a row of dolls lined up for a parade."

Ramona's face sagged and for a moment she lost control of herself as several tears of frustration joined the sweat on her face and rolled down her cheeks.

"Oh, no. How could I have been so stupid? I've led us along the wrong trail. This is Apache Leap. There isn't a way down from here. We'll have to backtrack several miles, and we just don't have time to do that before it gets dark." For the first time on the trip Ramona seemed to be at a loss as to what she should do next. She eased herself to the ground, put her head on her knees and said nothing more. Darby, Marcy, and Kevin seemed to have run out of strength to think up an answer to their latest problem. Even Brigadoon lay quietly with his head between his paws. The only sound was a low moan of the wind as it whistled through rocks of Apache Leap.

9

WATCH THAT FIRST STEP!

It was Kevin who finally broke the gloom that had settled over the tired hikers. "Well, for crying out loud, we can't just sit around doing nothing. It won't be long until dark. I don't think we ought to spend the night perched on the edge of this cliff."

"Can we climb down through the cracks in the rocks?" inquired Darby.

"No way," Kevin shot back. "I doubt even a good mountain climber could be sure of his footing. Say . . . I've just said the secret words—'mountain climber.' We can use the rope on my pack and rappel down!"

"Oh, neato!" Darby sounded glum. "The secret word for me is 'rappel.' Sounds like something you'd do in a boat."

Marcy's face brightened up when Kevin's idea sank in. "No, Darb, rappelling is a way of lowering yourself down a cliff by using a rope wrapped around your legs and back. It won't take you long to learn. Once you get the hang of it, it's sort of fun."

"Your idea is the best yet, but I think we'd better give

Darby a quick lesson before we start," Ramona said, brightening. She began helping Kevin straighten out the rope he was untying from beneath his pack.

"Let's practice on that small ledge over there." Kevin pointed to a rock outcrop that jutted about fifteen feet into the air. "There is a good place to tie the rope, and it's only a short drop to the ground."

The party was soon atop the ledge. Kevin and Ramona tightly tied one end of the rope around a rock and threw the other end over the ledge.

"First, face the rock and straddle the rope like this. Then, bring it up between your legs," Kevin instructed. "Now, with your left hand, move the rope around the front of your left leg, up over your left shoulder, and down your back. Grab the rope with your right hand."

"I feel as tied up as a Christmas present," muttered Darby, doing as he was told. "Okay, what now?"

"Hold the rope in front of your body with your left hand. Now lean back a little. Feel the rope tighten across your back? Use your left hand on the rope to help you stay upright as you go down."

"What do I do with my right hand?" Darby sounded bewildered.

"When you want to go down, loosen your grip on the rope just a little," Kevin replied. "Then, when you want to stop, grab the rope and pull it tight against your back."

Darby asked, "What happens if I lose my grip?"

"Don't worry," Kevin reassured him. "We have enough rope to use a belaying line on all of us as we go down the big cliff."

"Oh, no! Not another rope. What does a belaying line do?" Darby sounded frustrated.

"A belaying line is an extra rope around your waist. I hold the rope around a rock, and in case you lose your grip on the rope, the belaying line will keep you from falling."

"Well, here goes nothing." Darby's voice quivered just a little as he stood on the edge of the ledge and looked down. "Cripes, you mean that it's only fifteen feet to the bottom from here? Looks like a hundred!"

"Come on, Darb, you'll be fine," Ramona soothed. "I'll go below so that I can help if you need me. Marcy will be with me."

"Let's hope that I don't need any help," Darby came back. "I'm going to take it slow at first."

"All the time in the world, Darb," Kevin remarked calmly, wishing that Darby would get enough courage to begin.

Kevin watched anxiously as Darby gingerly loosened his grip on the rope in his right hand and started moving down. He was afraid to lean away from the face of the ledge, and as a result, his body dangled from the rope. Without the aid of his feet, Darby had to support his entire weight with his arms. Instead of rappelling, Darby found himself lowering his body hand over hand. His grip weakened. As he began to slide faster and faster, the rope started to burn his hands. Screeching in pain, Darby let go of the rope and plummeted to the ground, landing on his back with a resounding thud. He lay there, curled up in a ball, moaning softly to himself.

Ramona and Marcy ran quickly to his side, straightened out his legs, and carefully propped him up so that he would be more comfortable. "Where does it hurt most, Darby?" Marcy asked, biting her lips in sympathy.

"Oh, I'm not sure. My hands. My chest. Doggone . . . Why did I ever come on this danged trip?" Darby, who had propped himself up on his side, now slumped again to the ground.

Ramona got out one of her premoistened towels and swabbed Darby's hands, which were a bit raw from the rope burn. She then smoothed on some ointment from the first-aid kit. In a few minutes, Darby was able to stand and move about. The wind had been knocked out of him, but his pride had suffered more than anything.

By this time Kevin had scrambled down to where the others were gathered. "Sorry, sorry, sorry! That was my fault for not using the belaying line. The drop seemed like such a small one. Sure am sorry, Darb."

"No use crying now," Darby said, sitting up while he rubbed his shoulder.

"You aren't going to like this next suggestion, Darb, but you had better get back up there and practice at least one more time. The big cliff has only one step, but it's a mighty big one, if you get what I mean. I'll use the belaying line to be sure you don't fall again," Kevin spoke quietly but firmly.

"Yeah, I understand."

"Okay. This time, keep a tight grip on the rope with your right hand. And use your legs more to keep you away from the face of the cliff. I know that it doesn't seem natural to lean away from the rock. Force yourself to think about it as you go down. That way, you won't slide on the rope and burn your hands."

"Tie your bandanna around your right hand," Ramona added. "It will help keep the rope from rubbing the skinned places."

To everyone's surprise, Darby got up, brushed himself off, and muttered, "Well, I'll be danged if I'll be the one to hold up everyone else. Let's go." He climbed quickly back to the top of the small cliff and got the rope into position about his body. This time, the operation went without a hitch. Darby 'danced' down the side of the rocks and landed neatly on his feet.

"Nothing to it," he crowed cockily.

"Great," Kevin shouted, "but let's not get too swelled-headed yet. You have the biggest step ahead of you."

"I'll make it. No sweat," Darby shouted back.

"Well, let's get a move on," Ramona reminded everyone. "We've got a lot of rappelling to do before it gets any darker. Each of you had better wear your jacket to help prevent getting a rope burn on your back. I'll take Brigadoon down with me."

"Can you put him in your backpack?" Kevin asked.

"Might as well," Ramona answered. "Since Jake stole our food, I have extra space. I'll leave a few items with the rest of you. Will each of you please take some?"

"Sure 'nuff." Darby agreed.

Quickly the quartet moved to the edge of the cliff where Kevin found a huge rock with a notch that permitted him to tie the rope securely. Kevin also cut off part of the rope and, after fastening it to the rock, wrapped it about his shoulders. Ramona, with the belaying line tightly about her middle, was the first to go. She had no trouble, and she bounced her way easily to the ground despite her chubby figure.

Brig seemed to have enjoyed the trip down, for he ran around in small circles and made tiny leaps into the air when Ramona released him. She looked up and shouted, "All right, Darby, you're next."

Darby's head appeared slowly over the ledge of the cliff and then, quite suddenly, it was jerked back as he realized how far down he had to go.

"Might as well get started," he grumbled to himself. "The longer I stay up here, the farther it seems to down there." He stood poised for a moment on the edge, looking at his tender hands which he had wrapped in a spare pair of socks.

Kevin smiled at him. "You've got it made, Darb. Just lean away from the cliff and let the rope out slowly with your right hand."

Darby grinned weakly, gave the circle "okay" sign with his thumb and forefinger, and set out gingerly over the cliff's edge. Although he moved slowly, all went well. When he finally reached the bottom of the cliff, his wobbly legs couldn't support him, and he sank to the ground even before he took off the belaying rope.

"Okay, Darb. Up and at 'em," Ramona urged. "We've got to get Marcy and Kevin down."

Atop the cliff, Marcy prepared for the trip to the bottom. "Is the belaying rope knotted tightly?" asked Kevin.

"Looks okay to me," Marcy said. "Good luck! See you down below." Kevin nodded and smiled as his sister started her descent.

Things went well until about ten feet from the ground when Marcy pushed away from the rock face too vigorously. On the return swing, her legs buckled beneath her, and she crashed into the cliff. She cried out in pain. Her hands fell away from the ropes as her body went limp. Kevin felt the belaying line snap taut. He braced his legs to counteract the pull of Marcy's body. Slowly he lowered her to the ground. She lay there very still with the blood from her nose spreading quietly out on the ground.

Ramona ran over, followed by Darby. "Quick, Darby, help me get her onto her side with her head on her arm. Yell up to Kevin to get down here as fast as he can make it."

Darby shouted up to his cousin atop the cliff. It was only a few minutes until a panting Kevin hurried into the circle.

"How's she doing?" he asked, a worried look on his face. "Golly, I hope she's all right. I'd never forgive myself if something happened to her. I started this rappelling idea, but I sure wouldn't have if I had known this would happen!"

Ramona fanned Marcy's face with her handkerchief and reassured Kevin. "Stop worrying! This isn't your fault."

Darby hovered around looking helpless. "Isn't there anything I can do, Ramona?"

"Um h'm. Put a little water on your kerchief and bathe her face. Kevin, put your jacket under her head."

For a few minutes Marcy lay there quietly, moaning a little from time to time. Finally, she opened her eyes, grinned weakly, and said sheepishly, "Gosh, that last step was really a humdinger."

Kevin laughed in relief. "Yep, it sure was. What are you trying to do, Sis, break up our party?"

"No, just my face, I guess. Am I banged up very much?"

"Now that your nosebleed has stopped, you are as ugly as ever. I'm just kidding, Sis. Your eye looks a little black and blue, though. Can you walk okay?"

"Yes, I think so," Marcy got up slowly, stretched her arms and legs and moved around a bit. "I'll be all right. If the rest of you are ready, let's get going."

In a few minutes the party had started down the slope leading away from the cliffs. The sun was slipping behind the rocks and deep purple patches spread over the path ahead. Ramona brought the hikers to a halt near a rock outcrop with a small pool of water at its base.

"I think we ought to stop here for the night," she announced. "There is some firewood around. The water in this pond doesn't look too good, but it ought to do for washing our hands and faces. When it's all we've got, we can't be too choosy."

"I don't know about the rest of you, but I'm bushed," complained a pale and tired Darby as he slumped down against a rock and fell asleep almost immediately. Ramona and Kevin let him rest while they used the primus stove to heat some tea water.

When dinner was ready, they awakened Darby. The meal was a skimpy one. Ramona had found some jojoba bushes and had stripped them of their small but tasty nuts which everyone cracked between his teeth to get the seeds inside. The foursome shared two beef sticks, while a candy ball each served as dessert.

Kevin sipped his small ration of tea and smiled. "Well, it's better than nothing, but I sure would like to be tearing into one of those charcoal-broiled steaks Dad fixes."

"Oh, be quiet," Marcy moaned. "You aren't helping any."

"Yes," Ramona chimed in. "And just for that you can't have any more of these super delicious jojoba nuts."

"Gee! How lucky can I get?" Kevin grinned.

"You can get as lucky as I was today when I fell on my first rappel," Darby said. "From now on I'm going to stay away from cliffs I can't climb down."

"Well, at least we weren't forced to leap off them as some of my ancestors had to," Ramona remarked with a grim smile.

"I feel another Apache legend coming our way," Darby said with a sly grin.

"Not a legend, a true story this time," Ramona came back quickly. "About a hundred years ago my ancestors tried to regain the land that had been taken by the white man. The Apaches were outnumbered, so they fought in small bands that made daring, surprise raids on white settlements when they least expected them. My people were successful for a while. But at last they were driven back into these mountains. Here they were chased from one rocky stronghold to another by the whites who had been joined by many Pima warriors.

"Finally, the Apaches were stranded on these cliffs. Instead of surrendering, they retreated, fighting every inch of the way, until they could go no farther. The last step they took was when they leaped to their death rather than be captured."

The fire had died down, and the darkness surrounded the

tiny group as Ramona came to the end of her story. Everyone was quiet, partly because of the sadness of what they had heard, and partly because they were all very tired. Darby curled up in his sleeping bag, and soon fell soundly asleep. A quarter moon spread a pale light over the cliffs that towered above the sleepers. As Darby's subconscious took over, the cliffs slowly lost their stiff outlines, and each tall rock became a fierce Apache warrior fighting for his life. As each leaped over the cliff, he gave a blood-curdling cry which brought Darby upright in his sleeping bag shouting, "No! NO! NOT ME! I'm your friend!"

10

THE THUNDER GODS LEND A HAND

Dawn was barely breaking over the cliffs to the east when Kevin awoke. His nose was assailed by the smell of a fire and a strange aroma that drifted from it. He saw Ramona squatting by the blaze, and for a moment he had visions of her ancestors who had been building fires in this same area for hundreds of years. Watching as she stared into the embers, he thought he detected a note of deep concern, and he wondered if she knew of some danger of which he was unaware.

He slipped out of his sleeping bag and rubbed his eyes. Stumbling toward the girl, he asked, "What did you make the fire with, Princess Three Feathers, an old rubber tire?"

Ramona awoke from her reverie and turned to Kevin, smiling. "Oh, did the smell of this wonderful brew draw you to my campsite?" she asked.

"Brew? Smells more like chicken feathers. What is that in the kettle? You gonna poison us to save us from a slow death from starvation?"

"That, my paleface friend," said Ramona, "is what is commonly called Mormon tea. It smells a little odd, and it doesn't taste a whole lot better, but I thought it might be kind of invigorating to get us going this morning. I used parts of these bushes right here."

Kevin looked into the kettle. It seemed to be full of a liquid that did indeed look like tea, but it also contained small flat leaves and what appeared to be twigs. "Looks like it oughta be *in* the fire instead of *on* it," he laughed.

Before Ramona could defend her tea-making skill, she was interrupted by Darby singing in a surprisingly clear tenor voice, "Good morning, Mary Sunshine, and how are you today?"

Kevin blinked and began to laugh. Could this be Darby, who was usually unapproachable until at least fifteen minutes after he woke up?

Marcy opened her eyes to see what was causing the commotion and then burrowed deeper into her sleeping bag.

"Up! Up!" shouted Darby. "When I'm awake, nobody sleeps." He began to nudge Marcy's sleeping bag with his bare foot.

"No use fighting it, Marcy," said Kevin. "Time to get up. If we get an early start, we can put some miles behind us before it's too terribly hot."

Soon they were all seated around the fire, sipping the tea Ramona had concocted.

"No offense," said Darby, "but this is awful."

"It isn't the greatest," admitted Ramona, "but it's wet, and you'll need all the liquids you can get into your body before this day is over. Here, have a lemon drop. Hold it in your mouth when you drink the tea, and you'll think you're at some very fancy English castle. Sorry I didn't have time to make crumpets."

"That's a lot better," agreed Marcy, letting the tea pass over the lemon drop that Ramona had plopped into her mouth. "But I still wish I had some cold milk and cereal."

"We're in for a rough day," said Kevin. "We're going to need to find more water. I figure we'll get to the cowboy line shack sometime this afternoon, but we have less than a quart of water until then."

"Heck! We'll be all right," said Darby. "I'll give one of you my share of the water if you need it."

Ramona looked at Kevin, whose eyes mirrored her feelings. Could this be the same Darby who had begun the trip with them? Was this the complaining Eastern dude who hid food and grumbled almost constantly?

A few minutes later they were back on the trail, each moving along at an easy pace. The scenery had become especially beautiful. Entire cliffs of smooth rock seemed to have been painted with a soft coating of chartreuse, accented with spots of a deeper green. "How'd those rocks get to be that color?" asked Darby.

"The rocks aren't really green," answered Kevin. "They're coated with lichen, two very small plants that live together. The light green is the new growth and the dark green is the old lichen."

Looking around them, they marveled at the balanced rocks, boulders larger than houses that perched precariously on tall pillars of stone. From time to time they spied formations that were suggestive of Indian sentinels, constantly watching them as they moved along.

Plant life became scarcer and scarcer. What vegetation they saw was limited to various kinds of cacti and very dry bushes that seemed to have been dead for some time.

Although the hikers had gotten an early start, the sun ascended quickly, and before ten o'clock it must have been nearly one hundred degrees. Shady spots in which to stop for a rest became almost impossible to locate. The four of them found it more and more difficult to limit themselves to small sips from the canteen. Conversation ceased almost entirely, and occasionally they would find themselves spread out along the trail, out of sight of one another. The path had been gradually ascending, and their legs ached from exertion as they tried to keep up with one another.

"Brig isn't the only one who's panting now," gasped Marcy, her freckled face covered with sweat and dust. "Can't we stop for a while?"

"Let's try to make it around the next bend," answered Kevin, also breathing hard. "I think that rock outcrop might give us a little shade."

A few minutes later Kevin was sorry he had made the suggestion. The distance to the outcrop was deceiving, and it seemed to be taking forever to get there. Every muscle in his body ached, and his lungs felt as dry as the bushes around him. Looking back, he saw Marcy and Ramona struggling up the last rise, and he tried to encourage them.

"We're almost there now," he shouted, finding it difficult to force the words out. "Hang on."

Slowing down, he allowed Marcy and Ramona to catch up with him, and the three of them stumbled around the turn and sank slowly into the small spot of shade provided by the overhanging rocks.

They lay there without talking as their breath continued to come in great gasps. When a few minutes had passed, Ramona spoke haltingly. "Where's Darby? He was right behind us, I thought."

"He'll be here in a minute," said Marcy. "He's probably being smart and taking it slow."

Kevin rose to his feet. "I'm going back to look for him," he announced.

The girls watched him go, content to remain in the shade and let the tiredness seep out of their aching muscles.

Finally Marcy spoke. "What are you going to do with those feathers I've seen you picking up, Ramona?"

"Oh, did you notice that, Eagle Eyes? I thought I was being real sly," answered Ramona.

"Oh, I noticed it almost as soon as we started on this doggone safari, or whatever it is we're on," Marcy replied. "Are you making a headdress or something?"

"No, nothing like that," Ramona answered softly. "I'm afraid they're too small for anything very grand. I thought I might make some prayer sticks to leave for the Apache gods if we get through this adventure all right. It's the least I can do."

"Prayer sticks?" Marcy asked.

"Yes, you've probably seen them. They usually consist of sticks with strings attached to feathers or other ornaments."

Before Marcy could question further, she was interrupted by an excited shout from Kevin. "Ramona, come quick. Darby has passed out."

"Stay here," Ramona commanded Marcy. "Save your strength." Saying this she went racing down the trail.

After running about a hundred yards, she came upon Kevin bending over the prostrate form of Darby.

"It must be the heat," he said. "His skin is cold and damp. And look how rapid his breathing is. Quick, get his canteen open."

"Look at it," said Ramona, her eyes wide with wonder. "He's hardly taken a drop all day. I guess he meant it when he offered us his water this morning."

"Well, he's gonna need it now," replied Kevin. "Put some on a cloth and lay it on his forehead. I'll loosen his shirt. Do you think you can help carry him to the shady spot?"

"Sure," replied Ramona, taking Darby's legs as Kevin grasped him under the arms.

After a couple of stops, they came lugging Darby into the spot where Marcy waited.

"What's wrong? Is he gonna be all right?" asked Marcy excitedly.

"He has heat exhaustion," answered Kevin. "Get your hat and fan him. We need to get him cooled off as much as we can. He hasn't been drinking his water. He was saving it for us."

They laid Darby down carefully, and Marcy began to fan him as Ramona applied a damp handkerchief to his forehead. After a few seconds, Darby's eyes opened and he looked at Kevin, who was bending over him. Quickly his cousin placed the canteen to his lips and Darby began to drink thirstily.

"Easy," said Ramona. "Not too much right now. How are you feeling, Darby? You had us worried there for a minute."

"I'm okay. Kinda dizzy though," Darby answered. "Could I have some more water?"

"In a few minutes," said Ramona. "We're gonna need more water and soon," she said, turning to Kevin. "He's probably dehydrated, and the same thing could happen to the rest of us if we aren't careful."

"You're right," Kevin agreed, "but we shouldn't be more than a couple of miles from the cowboy line shack. There should be some water around there."

"I don't think we can take that chance," answered the Indian girl. "There may not be any water there, and two miles is a long way to go today. I'll bet the temperature's at least 115 degrees already."

"What do you think we should do then?" Kevin asked.

"I want you and Marcy to stay here with Darby. I'm going to find water," Ramona answered.

"I don't think it's a good idea for you to go off by yourself," replied Kevin. "Take Marcy with you, and I'll stay with Darby."

"No," said Ramona. "Marcy needs to get some rest. We

don't want anything else happening to her. I'll be all right. Believe me."

"Well," said Kevin slowly, "at least take Brig with you. He might help sniff out some water."

"Good idea," Ramona agreed. "Meanwhile, you take it easy and see that Marcy and Darby get lots of rest."

She gathered up the empty canteens and bottles and reached into her pack for the feathers she had been collecting. "Come on, Brig," she called. "Let's go find some water."

As Ramona went off, Darby raised himself on his elbows and began to look around. Then he sank back wearily. "I'm afraid I've made an awful lot of trouble," he said.

"No, you haven't," Marcy told him. "This stop gives us a good chance to rest."

"Thanks, Cuz," Darby said, trying to smile, "but I know I've been a real pain in the neck ever since I came to Arizona."

"Take it easy, pal," said Kevin, taking the hat from Marcy and continuing to fan Darby. "You got overheated. That's all. It could've happened to any of us."

"Do you think I'm gonna make it?" Darby asked weakly. "I really feel sick."

Marcy looked at Kevin.

"Sure you're gonna make it. All you have to do is get cooled off and get some rest," Kevin said. "Ramona will be back soon with lots of water and then we'll be on our way."

Darby put his hand out to Marcy and spoke softly. "Anyway, if I don't make it, I want to apologize for the way I acted. I really liked Arizona right from the start, but for some reason I just didn't want you guys to know it. I thought I had to play it cool and let you impress me. And I guess I thought you'd think I was chicken or something 'cause I didn't know how to ride a horse and do lots of things you can do. But you've been really great to me. I . . . I'm really sorry." Darby put his hand to his face.

Marcy's eyes filled with tears and she turned away from her cousin. Kevin patted Darby on the shoulder.

"Save your strength, pardner," he said. "We may be moving out pretty soon."

Kevin looked at his watch and anxiously surveyed the trail for some sign of Ramona.

"Better come and sit down," he said to his sister. "There's not much we can do now except wait."

Darby had closed his eyes. As he slept, his normal color returned and his breathing became regular.

When Ramona had left her friends, she had backtracked around them and headed in the direction from which they had come. Brig followed her obediently, seeming to sense that she knew where she was going. After walking about a mile, Ramona left the trail and followed a canyon that appeared to end abruptly at the base of a high cliff. But as the girl and the dog arrived at the cliff, they saw that what appeared to be a shadow was a small cleft in the rocks that led to a second canyon so narrow that even the midday sun barely penetrated it.

At the far end a spring trickled from the rocks into a small pool. The overflow from the pool disappeared once again into the rocks. Smelling the water, Brig barked twice and dashed to the spring. Ramona smiled as she watched the dog lapping up the water with his quick pink tongue, but she did not follow him. Taking the feathers from her pocket, she began to spread them in a large semicircle around the spring. After standing a moment to survey her work, she began to walk in and out of the feathered path, chanting softly in Apache.

"Great Thunder Gods," she intoned, "forgive us for entering your sacred grounds. We are foolish humans, but we do not come to take your gold. Soon we will be gone. I ask only that you share some of your water. I will never reveal any of your secrets."

After completing her ceremony, she gathered up the feathers, laid them in a pile, and struck a match to them. When they had burned themselves out, she scuffed the ashes into the dirt. Then she filled her canteens and bottles and, after taking a long drink from the pool, started back.

11

BEWARE OF FALLING ROCKS

As Ramona left the secret canyon, she carefully surveyed the surrounding area to be sure that she had not been observed. Although there had been no evidence of Jake since his early departure, more than once she had felt that their movement through the Superstitions had not gone unobserved. She had refrained from mentioning her feelings to the others, sensing that the heat, Marcy's accident, and Darby's illness had been enough to cope with. Seeing no sign of any humans, and with her canteens and bottles full, she left the larger canyon and was quickly back on the familiar trail, feeling refreshed from her spiritual experience and from the cooling drink of water.

When she had walked for perhaps ten minutes, she came to an area where the path divided, one way going up a dead-end canyon. As Ramona's eyes followed this path, she saw the reflection of the sun on some shiny object midway up the side of one of the canyon walls. Although she realized that the flash might have come from a tin can or some kind of mineral, she studied the terrain carefully. Just as she was about to move on, a small avalanche began in the area from which the reflection had come.

Well, that could be a mountain goat up there, she thought to herself, but I saw the sun reflecting on a pair of lenses, and goats don't wear glasses.

After looking at the distant spot a few seconds more and being unable to see any movement, she continued up the trail toward her friends, but her pace was faster now. She knew that those waiting for her were very thirsty, but she had another reason for her urgency. She was certain that for some reason Jake was tracking them.

Ramona's return was greeted with relief for her safety and with gratitude for the plentiful water that she came lugging up the trail. Marcy was so excited at seeing her friend that she did not notice Ramona had returned from the opposite direction from which she had departed.

Kevin was aware of her doubling back, but he decided to keep quiet, knowing from past experience that the remarkable Indian girl always had a good reason for her actions.

Marcy's shrieks of delight at seeing Ramona and Kevin's "Good girl, Ramona!" awakened Darby, who sat up and declared that he "felt like a new man." Kevin insisted that Ramona sit down, and Marcy proceeded to fan her with her hat.

"Now that we have plenty of water, I want everyone to take a salt tablet," said Kevin. "We still have about two tough miles to go, and we don't want anyone else getting sick."

"I feel like I could eat a baked owl," said Darby. "I sure hope there's some food at the line shack."

"What would you say to some jackrabbit?" laughed Ramona, pointing up the trail. The others joined in the mirth as they saw Brigadoon happily chomping on a young jackrabbit that he had caught sometime on the return trip.

Nearly two hours later the four hungry hikers arrived at

their destination, the line shack. The two-mile walk had been grueling, but sustained by plenty of water and the knowledge that they would soon find some wholesome food, they had been able to cover the distance with a minimum of discomfort.

The line shack, a small frame structure, was built against a cliff in a small canyon. Constructed of pine boards brought in on horseback, its flat roof sloped from front to back. Strips of wood nailed over the cracks between the boards and shutters on the lone window made the shack weatherproof. The cabin had been built by ranchers in the area as a stopping place and emergency headquarters for cowboys to use during roundup in the vast wilderness. Two paloverde trees and several ocotillo plants grew near the shack. As rough and rustic as it was, to the hikers it represented civilization and protection after days of being in the open.

"Look!" cried Darby. "It's the Superstition Hilton!"

The other three began to laugh. Marcy threw off her backpack and flopped down on the ground. "Somebody ring for the bellhop," she giggled. "And tell the maid to draw my bath."

"And call room service," Ramona added. "I'd like one of everything on the menu."

As their laughter subsided, they lay catching their breath and surveying the shack.

Finally Kevin rose and walked to the cabin. A hasp on the door was secured by a heavy padlock. After rattling the door a couple of times, he walked to the shuttered window as the others watched anxiously. Seeing no lock, he pushed on the wooden panels, but they were locked from inside.

"What's the penalty for breaking and entering in Arizona?" asked Darby, not joking this time but with a look of deep concern on his grimy face.

"I don't know," Kevin answered, "but this is an emergency and we've got to find a way to get into this shack." As he sat on a rock thinking, he was joined by Brigadoon, who nuzzled his head against Kevin's arm, hoping to receive a friendly pat. At first Kevin brushed him off, but then as Brig started to walk away, Kevin called to him, "Come here, Brig. Let me feel your muzzle."

Brig scampered back, and Kevin knelt to pick him up. "Hey! His face is wet!" Kevin exclaimed. "He's found some water around here."

The others rose to their feet. "Where is it, Brig?" asked Marcy. "Come on, show it to us."

Pleased with the attention, Brig began to bark and then ran to a ravine behind the cabin, followed by Darby and Marcy, who found him standing proudly by a clear, trickling spring with a small, clear pool at its base.

After drinking deeply and washing some of the trail dust from their faces, they returned to the shack and reported their find.

"That's great," said Kevin. "We'll be in good shape now if we can just get into this cracker box of a cabin."

"You know," said Darby thoughtfully, "I don't think every cowboy who's out looking for stray cows is gonna carry a key with him. I'll bet the key to that lock is hidden somewhere around here. What are the places people usually hide keys?"

"Under the doormat," was Marcy's quick reply.

"In a flowerpot," laughed Ramona.

"Very funny," said Kevin quietly. "Now that we've got all the ridiculous things out of the way, how about some serious ideas?"

"Okay," replied Darby, rising and running his hand over the top of the door jamb. "How about right . . . *Here!*" With an unbelieving look, he turned to face the group, a tarnished brass key in his hand.

"Fantastic," said Marcy, jumping up and down. "Quick, let's see if it fits the lock."

"Stand back," said Darby grandly. "Let Houdini Driscoll perform the miracle of the ages." He inserted the key into the padlock and with a loud snap it opened. Removing the lock from the hasp, Darby pushed the door inward.

At once the four young people stampeded through the opening and into the shack.

"Raise that bar and open the window to let in more light." said Kevin.

As Ramona performed the chore, the others surveyed the small interior. Two bunk beds lined one side of the cabin, and a rough fireplace filled most of the opposite side. Along the back wall, rough planks formed shelves that held perhaps thirty cans of assorted meats, fruit, and vegetables. A tall tin held coffee, and another was marked "flour."

"Boy, are we gonna eat today," said Marcy. "We can live like kings."

Kevin put his hand on her shoulder and spoke. "Before we go opening any of these cans, we have to talk about something." The others looked at him with puzzled expressions.

"First of all," he went on, "we have to be careful about how much we use. Somebody may come along who is even worse off than we are, and a can of beans might mean life or death to him."

"That's quite true," Darby agreed, "but there's a lot of food here, and we'll leave more than enough for whoever comes after us."

"Okay," said Kevin, "just so we all know we can't make absolute pigs of ourselves. The second thing is that we can't just take things. We have to pay for them."

"I don't have any money," moaned Marcy. "Who takes money to go hiking in the Superstitions?"

"I don't think any of us has any money," replied Kevin, looking at Darby, "but we could leave something of value in return."

Darby's hands went to his pants pockets and he turned away from Kevin.

"Darby, do you have anything of value we could leave?" Kevin asked.

"What are you talking about?" Darby questioned sheepishly.

"Well, I'll leave the answer to that question up to you, but we're all going to get awfully hungry waiting for you to decide."

Darby eyed the cans of food longingly as the others watched. From his right pocket he slowly withdrew the gold nugget Jake had left. As he placed it on the makeshift cupboard, the others rushed to examine the cans.

"Oh, boy, peaches," said Marcy.

"And tomato juice," added Ramona.

Suddenly Kevin, hearing a sound from above them, threw his weight against the other three, who fell domino style to the floor. Before they could protest, a huge boulder crashed through the opposite side of the cabin roof. Recovering quickly, they jumped over the hole the rock had torn in the plank floor and dashed outside. Only Kevin, who was the first one out, saw the quick movement of a bearded man high on the cliff above the cabin.

12

PRISONER OF WAR

"Boy, that was a close call," said Darby. "Why did they build this cabin so close to the cliff anyway?"

"That's one balanced rock that didn't stay balanced," Marcy added.

"I wouldn't be surprised if our friend Jake rolled it down on us," laughed Darby.

Kevin glanced at Ramona and a look of understanding passed between them. "Just a little avalanche," Kevin said. "I'll go back in and get some food while the rest of you get a fire started under that rock outcrop over there. Falling rocks can't get to us there."

After their first real meal for some time, they sat around the fire they had built under the rock ledge. As night began to fall, they spread their bedrolls out and all except Kevin soon fell asleep.

Early the next morning, refreshed from the food and rest and an old-fashioned water fight at the pool, they were back on the trail. This would be the last leg of their trek to meet Larry.

Several times Ramona and Kevin stopped to consult the map, wanting to make absolutely certain that they were on the right trail. It was during one of these consultations when they were alone that the Indian girl told Kevin about seeing Jake on the side of the canyon the previous day. When he heard this, Kevin knew that he had not imagined seeing Jake on the cliff after the rock had fallen on the cabin.

"I don't know if he's crazy or what," said Kevin, "but it's clear that he's more than just a thief who would steal water and food from people. I don't think that boulder fell by accident. I think he's trying to kill us."

"But what reason would he have? Didn't Darby tell him that we're just out here to meet Larry?"

"Yes," answered Kevin, "and I've been thinking about that. Darby also told him that we had a map. If he's as loco as he seems, he may think it's a treasure map and that we're trying to find the Lost Dutchman Mine."

"But you can't just go around killing everyone who is looking for it," answered Ramona.

"Think about how many people have been killed out here just for that very reason," Kevin replied. "And I also think that you have something to do with Jake's concern, Ramona. Maybe he thinks that you're another Ken-tee and that you are going to lead us to the gold."

"That sounds logical, I guess, but I think I've made it clear to you about how I feel about the Superstitions. I think the gold must remain here."

"We all know that, but if Jake does, he doesn't believe it."

With that, they quickened their steps and joined the others.

"Boy, I can't wait to tell Larry about our trip," said Marcy. "All he's doing is looking at pictures on rocks while we met Jacob Walz's grandson, rappelled down a cliff, and nearly died from starvation."

"Well, he probably thinks that what he's doing is pretty exciting too," said Ramona. "But I agree that this has been quite a trip. And it's not over yet. Anyway, we'll find out in just a few minutes. Larry's campsite should be in that next canyon just to the right."

Ramona's map-reading ability proved to be correct, for they were soon in the box canyon Larry had designated.

"Now," said Kevin, "he should be working under that huge balanced rock right over there."

With Brigadoon leading the way, the small band plodded wearily in the direction in which Kevin had pointed. When they were directly beneath the huge boulder, Marcy pointed up the trail and sang out, "Look, there's where his campfire was. He's got to be around somewhere."

Darby and Kevin broke into a run and arrived at the campsite before the girls. "Look! Here's his backpack," shouted Darby.

"Yeah," Kevin agreed, "and this is his bedroll. He's probably close by somewhere."

They were joined by the girls. Everyone dropped backpack and bedroll on the ground and sat down to await Larry's return.

"He's really gonna be surprised that we came to meet him," said Marcy.

When a half hour had passed and Larry did not return, Kevin spoke. "When I count to three, let's all yell 'Larry.' That way, wherever he is, he will probably hear us. Okay. Let's go. One, two, three."

"LARRY!" they shouted in unison.

"Again. One, two, three."

"LARRY!" they shouted again and again for several minutes.

"Wherever he is, he can't hear us," said Darby. "I think

we'd better go look for him. He could have fallen or something."

"I think you're right," Kevin agreed. "You and Ramona go up this canyon and Marcy and I will take this one. Mark your trail as you go. We'll meet back here in half an hour."

As they were about to part, the stillness of the late afternoon was broken by a loud explosion that reverberated from canyon to canyon and echoed again and again.

"World War III has started," said Darby, trying to hide the fear that his visibly pale face showed.

"What is it really?" asked Marcy. "Is it the Apache gods?"

"No, Little One," Ramona assured her. "I think it's a safe guess that somebody is doing some dynamiting on the other side of that ridge there." She pointed to a rocky mesa several hundred yards away.

"It can't be Larry," said Kevin, "because he didn't take any explosives with him. But I'll bet that's where he is. He probably just wanted to watch the fireworks."

"Let's go see," shouted Darby, and they were soon headed toward the distant ridge where a mushroom of smoke and dust now rose as a beacon to guide them. Their tiredness forgotten, they moved faster than they had all day, so anxious were they to see Larry and to find out about the explosion. Even though the way was mostly uphill, they covered the area in less than half an hour, with Kevin in the lead by several feet.

At the very top of the rise Kevin slipped, and as he pulled himself up, the others began to laugh. Kevin looked over the top of the hill and then quickly turned around and placed his fingers to his lips.

"What's up?" Darby whispered.

"Get down and stay down," Kevin hissed. "Now, one at a time, each of you look over the top here. I don't think you're gonna like what you see."

As each of the other three looked, they turned around and faced Kevin silently, their eyes wide with fright. Having caught his breath, Kevin once again peered down into the valley below. What he saw was Larry, his close-cropped blond hair wet with perspiration, seated on the ground under a paloverde tree, his arms tied behind him. Near him was a huge dark-skinned woman and a red-faced man. The woman's deeply resonant voice could be heard plainly as she spoke.

"How'd the dynamiting go?" she asked. "You certainly kicked up enough dust. It can probably be seen for miles around. Sure hope the Forest Service doesn't come poking around here."

"What makes you think it hasn't already?" asked the man, pointing to Larry. "You don't believe that story about him being a student do you?"

"Yes, I believe it," the woman replied. "I had a look at his wallet while you were gone. He's a student all right, but I found something else very interesting." She unfolded a map and showed it to the man. "What do you make of these strange marks on here?"

"Looks like some kind of code," the man said. "Might be worth looking into."

Larry, who had been straining his muscular body against the ropes, spoke up. "I told her already that I'm just looking for petroglyphs. I'm taking pictures for an archaeology class. I'm not trying to jump your claim."

"How come all these strange markings on this map then?" the woman asked.

"That's my kid brother's work," Larry answered. "I think he wanted to make the trip a little more exciting so he added a few touches here and there to my map."

"A likely story," the man sneered.

Darby looked at Kevin who was shaking his head in em-

93

barrassment for what he had done to the map and for the trouble it was causing his brother. Darby started to speak, but held his tongue, after looking at Kevin.

Leaving his vantage point, Darby carefully slid several feet back down the hill, a look of determination on his face. He motioned to the others, who quickly joined him, and then he spoke. "We've got to get Larry out of there," he said. "That tree's not giving him much shade and it's darned hot down there."

"Yeah, and did you see that gun the woman has?" asked Marcy. "She means business."

"What do you have in mind?" questioned Ramona, sensing a new side to Darby.

"We need to get them away from Larry somehow," Darby replied. "Then we can slip down and untie him. Anyone got any ideas?"

"Maybe if we wait here awhile," offered Ramona, "that man and woman will go over to where they are blasting and we can sneak down and untie Larry."

"That's a possibility," Darby answered, "but it looks to me as if they're keeping him pretty well guarded."

"I wonder," said Kevin, pointing, "if we could go over there a ways and roll down some rocks and distract them for a while."

"I'm afraid they'd see us if we did," said Darby.

"Maybe we should just try the direct approach and go down and talk to them and convince them that we're not looking for gold and they'll let Larry go," Ramona suggested.

As they were considering Ramona's idea, the silence was violently broken by a series of gunshots from near the area where the dynamiting had taken place. Bullets could be heard ricocheting off canyon walls and voices shouted, "Get down!" and "We're being bushwacked!"

Almost immediately, more shots were fired in return and

the unmistakable voice of the woman guarding Larry rang out. "It's that McSorley bunch. I knew they'd be back to cause trouble. Quick, Sam, let's get over there and help out our boys."

Darby cautiously peeked over the top of the rise and watched as the woman and the man ran toward the dynamite area, leaving Larry tied, but unguarded.

"Now's our chance, Kevin. Let's go get Larry," Darby whispered fiercely.

Before Kevin could consider the wisdom of his cousin's suggestion, Darby was over the crest and heading down toward the campsite.

"You girls stay here," Kevin commanded. "If we're not back in ten minutes, find Larry's campsite and wait for us. Keep Brig with you."

Kevin quickly followed Darby down the hill, keeping his eyes on the departing man and woman. Intent upon helping their fellow miners, the two did not turn around. Ducking and running, Darby and Kevin raced pell-mell to Larry's rescue.

As he watched his captors depart, Larry renewed his struggle to free himself of the ropes that bound him to the paloverde tree. So concentrated were his efforts, he was not aware of Darby's approach until his cousin knelt behind him, pulled out a pocketknife, and began to saw away at the rope.

"Take it easy, old pal," said Darby calmly. "We'll have you out of here in a jiffy."

Larry turned, and a broad smile lit up his sweat-streaked face as Kevin joined them.

"Come on, let's get out of here before they come back," said Larry, taking the boys' arms as he rose to his feet. All three of them began to race back to where Ramona and Marcy awaited.

They had gone only a few feet when a bullet slammed into

95

the dirt in front of them, forcing them to take cover behind a rock.

"Where'd that bullet come from?" Darby asked. "I think everyone out here has gone absolutely mad."

"Look up on that rock there," said Larry, pointing. "Whoever he is thinks we're some of the miners, and is trying to pin us down."

As he spoke, they saw the dark woman rise, put her rifle to her shoulder and fire. The man on the rock stood silhouetted against the sky for an instant and then plummeted headfirst down the hill.

"Pretty good shooting for an opera singer," said Larry.

"What?" asked Kevin.

"I'll tell you later," Larry answered. "Let's get the heck out of here now. Come on!"

All three boys rose and ran in a zigzag pattern to the next big rock on their path up the hill. Another shot rang out, and dust and bits of rock scattered about them as the bullet p-tinged off a boulder.

"Everybody, down! She's spotted us!" Darby barked.

More shots rang out. The bullets seemed to be coming from all directions. Cautiously, Larry peered over the top of the protecting rock. He could see the woman and the man called Sam. They too were hiding behind a boulder held down by someone firing from the cliffs above them.

"It's now or never," Larry said. "Keep as low as you can. Let's go up this way."

"No! We can't!" Kevin shouted, pulling at his brother. "The girls are up this way."

"Girls?" Larry asked, a strange look on his face.

"Marcy and Ramona," said Darby. "They're waiting for us over the crest and to our right."

"Oh, no," said Larry. "Well, let's find them and get them away from this gunfight."

One by one the boys left their place of safety and continued their zigzag course up the hill. From time to time shots rang out, but it was difficult to tell who was shooting. Little by little they worked their way to the top.

Kicking rocks in all directions, they dived over the crest of the hill. As Darby, who was bringing up the rear, jumped over the top to safety, a bullet tore up the ground behind him. But they were safe, and, smiling and panting, they slid down the hill toward the happy girls.

13

DRY BONES

Larry, Darby, and Kevin, crouching low as they ran, came around the corner of the large rock where Ramona and Marcy were standing.

"Larry," shrieked Marcy. "Oh, Larry, it's great to see you. Are you all right?"

"I'm a little roughed up, but I'll live," panted Larry as he hugged his sister.

Even Ramona, breaking her usual calm, threw her arms about Larry and exclaimed, "It's great that you are safe, Larry."

"I'm twice as glad as all of you put together that I'm alive," beamed Larry. "And where did you find this tiger named Darby? He's not what I remember from the last visit two years ago. I don't think I'd be out of that woman's hands yet if it hadn't been for him. Darby, I'll never forget how brave you were."

Darby had had time to recover his wind and to rethink the events of the past half hour. He hadn't lived with this new part of his personality long enough to be sure that he understood what it was really like. As a result, Darby only smiled.

"What I don't understand is why any of you happened to be here at all to save me," remarked Larry. "I was supposed to meet you at the entrance to Peralta Canyon, and now you pop up in the middle of a gunfight. Is there something I should be worrying about?"

Ramona, Kevin, and Marcy all talked at once, telling Larry how they had decided to meet him on the trail or at the line shack. They also hurriedly told him about their problems, including the theft of their food, and ended with the narrow escape that morning when the rock crashed through the line shack.

When everyone had calmed down a bit, they started to plan their next move.

"We are pretty safe here for a while, provided we don't get in the way of a ricochet bullet," Larry said.

"Where do we go from here?" Darby asked.

"Looks as though you ought to head for a clothing store," Kevin laughed, putting his finger through a hole in Darby's left shirt sleeve.

"Holy mackerel!" exclaimed Darby. "I didn't know the bullet came that close. Wait'll the guys back in Ohio hear about this!"

"I don't think that we ought to stay here very long," Larry said. "Let's go back to my campsite so I can pick up my gear."

"Good," said Kevin, "we left our packs near yours."

Crouching as low as they could, but still moving quickly, they beat a hasty retreat from the scene of the firing. About fifty yards farther along, they rounded a corner in the trail and, safe from zinging bullets, they collapsed on each side of the path for a rest.

"Whew!" said Darby, as they finally stood up to move along. "You westerners really take your mining claims seriously, don't you?"

"Well," said Larry, "we've seen reports about these gunfights in the Phoenix papers from time to time. I'll have to admit, though, it's far more exciting to be in the middle of one than to be reading about it."

About an hour later, the young people had returned to Larry's camp, had some canned food for lunch, and were ready to set out on the homeward journey. Larry gathered the group around him and suggested, "I think we ought to move up higher, off the canyon floor, so that we can look about and see just where we are."

"Good idea," Darby agreed. "If any of the gun-toting squatters are following us, we can spot them before they overtake us."

Ramona pointed up the side of the canyon. "There's a small, almost invisible trail leading up this way."

"Okay, let's take that one. Looks as good as any." Larry set a rather rapid pace up the rocky path.

Twenty hot and sweaty minutes later, Marcy called out, "Hey, let's take a break. I've had it for a few minutes."

The party squatted in what shade they could find. Kevin, leaning against a scrubby paloverde tree, looked over the surrounding rocky, barren landscape. Suddenly his body tensed, and he pointed up the hillside.

"What is that up there? It looks like a cave opening."

They all got to their feet and squinted up at the rocks, which reflected the glare of the sunshine.

"I think you are right!" Darby exclaimed.

"It's either a cave or an old mine," Larry said thoughtfully. "Sometimes, prospectors started digging and then just left a hole behind when they thought the mine was worthless. It looks as though it is just a little ways from the trail. It would give us a cool place to rest for a while."

The party, at a somewhat slower pace to accommodate for the steeper trail, set out again. Finally the path leveled off, and the hikers found themselves following the contour of the hillside. When they reached the place in line with the cave, they scrambled up the rocks for about twenty-five yards and halted in front of a small opening.

"You were right, Larry," said Ramona. "It is an old mine. Look at the funny shape of the entrance."

Instead of being just a hole chiseled into the rock, the entrance was tapered, larger at the top and narrower at the bottom. There were no timber supports, and the mine roof depended entirely upon the rocky walls for its support.

"What do you think, Larry?" asked Kevin. "Can we go inside and explore?"

"I don't know," said Larry. "I'm not sure that it is the safest thing to do. A lot of these tunnels are very old and the construction is lousy. It could cave in at any time. A few years ago, a prospector named Al Morrow lost his life in one of these old places. He was trying to make the side of the mine wider and the whole mess came tumbling down on him."

"Oh, come on," begged Kevin. "Let's go in for a little way. We won't be doing any digging. If it looks dangerous, we can come back out right away."

"Okay, but let me lead," said Larry. "I think I can tell how safe it is better than any of the rest of you."

Darby gave a little bow and, passing his hand in front of his chest, smirked, "Be our guest, Larry."

When everyone had dug his flashlight out of his bag, Larry led the party into the mine opening. He had to bend his neck just a bit, but the others stood upright with just a little headroom to spare.

"Ouch," cried Marcy as she stumbled over something in the dark. "What in the dickens is that?" She shone her light at her feet and picked up what looked like a horseshoe.

"Say, that's a rather strange-looking horseshoe," exclaimed Kevin.

"Sure is," echoed Larry. "Look at the way the ends curve outward. It's too small for a horse. Probably a mule shoe. It certainly was handmade, judging from the rough places in the iron. It looks very much like some I saw in a Mexican museum last year."

"Say, do you think this might have come from one of the mules used by the Peralta miners when they stripped gold from this area?" asked Kevin.

"Can't say for sure," replied Larry, "but I do know that the Mexicans used mules to help haul ore out of the mines."

With this small but exciting discovery, the party hurried deeper into the mine. As they made their way along, the beams from their flashlights accented the scars made in the rock by the men who had dug there long ago.

Larry shone his light ahead, and as its beam suddenly fell on a blank wall, he commented, "Looks as though we've reached the end of the passageway. The mine must have been a dud. I haven't seen anything yet that looks as though it would have any gold in it."

Ramona swung her light around at the bottom of the wall. "Oh, oh," she exclaimed. "This was a close call. Look at that!"

Darby whistled. "I'll be darned. There's a shaft leading almost straight down into the rock. We almost fell into it! Look, there's a log leaning against the side."

They all gathered carefully around the hole and shone their lights downward. The log, about twenty feet long and notched with a series of deep cuts in one side, came to rest on another level.

"It looks like a kind of ladder," said Kevin.

"You're right, Kev," Larry said. "The Mexicans used to load baskets of ore on their backs and carry them from the lower levels to the outside by using these ladders. Are all of you game to go down? I think it's safe enough. Let me go first and, if the ladder holds, you can follow."

Larry made his way slowly down the ancient ladder while the others lighted his way. Soon, all were safely on the lower level, Brig riding down in Kev's emptied pack. The tunnel was smaller than the main one above.

Larry warned, "We must be very careful and mark every turning point we make. It wouldn't do to get lost now."

Larry led the way, and even Brig seemed to catch the spirit of the occasion as he bounced along in the circle of Larry's flashlight. Suddenly, the tunnel jogged to the right. Brig made the turn and then came scurrying back letting loose low growls, alternating with sharp barks.

"What's up, Brig?" asked Kevin. "He usually doesn't get that excited unless he has found something unusual."

"Okay, Brig, let's go," urged Larry. But Brig was obstinate. He refused to budge an inch. "Guess I'll have to see for myself."

The young man moved cautiously around the corner, flashed his light ahead, and came to a sudden halt. He let out a low whistle and shouted, "Come here, gang, and see what Brig discovered!"

As the beams moved around the corner of the tunnel, they converged on a set of yellowed human bones, the skeleton of a man. It lay in a position on its side with the knees pulled up against the rib cage. Most of the clothing had long since rotted away, although there was a buckle on a frayed belt, and two boots through which bony toes protruded. A rusty knife lay to one side. Wire-rimmed glasses lay crushed beneath one side of the skull. Strangest of all was a metal box clutched in the right hand of the skeleton. It was partly hidden by the rib cage as though the owner, when he had died, had tried to keep his object a secret from the rest of the world.

Larry bent over and examined the skull. "Here's something strange! Did you notice that this side is bashed in a bit?

It looks as though he suffered a blow that may have killed him."

"Do you think that he might have fallen down that crazy ladder?" asked Marcy. "If he did, he probably crawled in here and couldn't go any farther."

"But why was he all the way down here in the first place?" asked Darby.

"Probably exploring, just as we are," Kevin suggested.

"There must be something very valuable in that box," offered Ramona. "He didn't bring anything else into the mine with him. Evidently he wasn't about to leave it outside. Maybe if we opened the box, it would tell us who he was and what he was doing here."

"Good idea," said Larry. "Let's take a look." He gently moved the rib cage aside and picked up the metal box.

Ramona, sensing that everyone was more than a little nervous suggested, "Why not go back outside? We can see better in the daylight."

Everyone hastened to agree. Soon the group found itself blinking in the bright hot sunlight while Larry broke open the lock on the box by striking it a sharp blow with the point of a rock. They all squatted about him as he gently removed a long envelope of waterproof cloth which he carefully unwrapped. Inside was a folded square of heavy brown paper that seemed to be in excellent condition.

Larry whistled under his breath. "Well, what do you know! It's a map, a very old map, dated 1890."

"That's more than eighty-five years ago," muttered Darby. "How did this man get the map? Why did he bring it here? What does the map mean? It is sort of hard to make out."

"Well," said Ramona, "you remember the legend about old Walz's death. He wasn't conscious the last couple of days before he died. If this map is genuine, the fellow, whoever he is, may have stolen it from the Dutchman."

Kevin carried the theory further. "I'll bet this fellow was hunting for the mine, and stopped in here to rest. While exploring, he probably fell down the shaft just as Marcy said."

"Sounds reasonable," said Larry. "I'm not sure yet what the map means. But look at the W in the lower corner." Larry tapped his teeth with his thumbnail while he thought about what he saw. "You know what? This could just turn out to be the most lucky day of our lives!"

Ramona stood slowly, turned, and looked into the heart of the Superstitions. She sighed and said, almost to herself, "I wonder, Larry, if this mightn't turn out to be the most *unlucky* day of our lives."

14

ESCAPE AT NIGHT

Larry didn't seem to hear Ramona's remark. He turned back to the map with great excitement. "Well, gang, what do you think it means?"

Marcy, Kevin, and Darby huddled around the map with Larry. Only Ramona stood to one side and did not join in as the others tried to decipher the markings on the paper.

"I wonder what the big mountain or rock on the right side means? It certainly must represent something very large," Kevin said.

"Well, it could be," said Larry. "On the other hand, it may have been drawn large because the person who made the map was standing close to the rock. Come to think about it, though, the big peak must represent the biggest mountain in this area. Notice the name attached to it, 'El Sombrero.' That's Spanish for 'The Hat.' Seems to me that's the name the early Mexicans gave to Weaver's Needle."

Darby peered at the huge rock formation in the distance and said, "Well, there's the Needle, but it sure doesn't look like the drawing on the map."

"No," said Kevin, "but it might if we moved to a different position and looked at it from a different angle."

"How about that Spanish phrase on the other side of the map?" asked Darby. "What does *'para los caballos'* mean?"

Larry translated, "For the horses. H'mmm . . . look at the drawing. Two peaks with a sloping connection between. Looks somewhat like a saddle. Saddles are for horses. So maybe we are looking for two connected hilltops shaped like a saddle opposite Weaver's Needle."

Kevin borrowed Larry's topographic map, spread it out on the ground, and hunched over it, trying to locate some of the formations drawn on the old map.

"Let's see if we can find a saddle on the government map," he said. "Yes, here's one. Saddle Bluffs, and it is opposite Weaver's Needle."

"Well, at least we have something on it figured out," sighed Marcy. "I don't understand what some of those other drawings on the old map mean. Look at the one side of the saddle. There is something that looks like a Y with a snake for a tail that ends with a G in the center of a circle. And all of that is beside an X."

"Well," said Larry, "if this map was drawn by old Jacob Walz, he'd be trying to remind himself of where he found the gold mine. So, the G must mean gold, and the X must be the location of the mine. I'm not sure what the Y means. It doesn't seem to be part of a word. It could indicate some sort of a rock formation."

"Say, Larry, I think that you are doing great," said Kevin, "but we still don't know anything about the letter and number over Weaver's Needle. The J and the 4 are opposite a big circle."

"Maybe the circle stands for the sun," Marcy said.

"Yeah, I think you are right," Darby replied. "And the J could stand for Jake, June, or July. I'll bet the letter is for one of the months, and the 4 stands for the day of the month."

Kevin looked thoughtful. "Maybe the four stands for the time of day, since the number is opposite what we think is the sun."

"Sounds as though you have something there, Kev," replied Larry. "Maybe what we want to find is a place on the side of Saddle Bluffs where the sun will shine at four o'clock over Weaver's Needle onto a Y. Near that place we'll find the gold mine."

"Larry," said Kevin, "I wish I could think of a better explanation, but right now I don't think that I can. There are a couple of other things on the map we haven't figured out yet, though."

"You probably mean that big arrow at the bottom, and the arrows pointing from east to west and from north to south," Larry came back. "My first guess is that the big arrow points to north. I'm not sure about the east-west, north-south symbols."

Darby looked quizzical. "But if we move the map so that the big arrow points north," he said, "then the drawings on the map are not matched with actual features on the ground as we see them from here. I don't think the large arrow points north. There's got to be something else."

"Hadn't we better figure out what it is before we go any further with our plans?" asked Marcy.

"Oh, I don't know," Larry replied. "We won't get much accomplished just squatting here in the hot sun. Why not move on toward Saddle Bluffs and scout around there? Something may come to us as we hike along."

Marcy looked hesitant. "Do you think that we have enough food to last us while we go roaming around the mountains without a plan?"

"Well, I think we have," said Kevin, "as long as we don't make hogs of ourselves. We still have some stuff left from the cowboy line shack. What do you think, Ramona?"

Ramona had remained silent during the translation of the symbols of the map. Now she turned to the group, and with a note of despair in her voice spoke rapidly, "I think that all of you are being very greedy and very foolish. Already we have had our food stolen. Larry's been captured, and we've almost been killed by that 'accident' in the line shack. Still you aren't willing to listen to what I think is the message from my gods who make their home in these mountains. They are telling us to stay away and not to try to find the Apache gold. If we do, more horrible things may happen. I love you all very dearly as friends, and I beg of you not to go on. I have a feeling in my heart that things will not turn out right."

This was the first time that the others had heard Ramona speak so long and so seriously about anything. For many seconds they stood and looked at her, torn between their affection for their friend and the desire to locate the fabulous gold mine that now seemed nearer than ever.

"But, Ramona," Kevin replied, "we don't intend to steal the gold. I'd be happy if we just found the mine."

"I don't know how happy you'd be," Ramona replied seriously. "A lot of people have searched for the gold, and they have either died or they were bitterly disappointed."

This discussion continued for some time. Finally, against Ramona's wishes, they decided to push on to find the mine.

Ramona sighed and said with a tone of resignation, "You are my friends and I won't leave you in the middle of the wilderness. I'll go with you, but I want you to know that I'm not happy in doing so, nor do I think that the Apache Thunder Gods are pleased."

With this distressing statement hanging over them, the party got their gear together and started out silently on the trail. The hot afternoon sun broiled down on them as they picked their way slowly among the rocks toward Saddle

Bluffs. The twin mountains were only a few short miles away, but the heat of the day caused the young hikers to stop many times until they finally slumped down in the shade of a large rock that partially hid a small spring. After sloshing water over their faces and arms and filling their canteens, they stretched out on the ground for a short siesta.

Marcy, her face flushed, seemed particularly tired. She fell quickly into a deep but fitful sleep despite the heat of the afternoon. A few times she moaned and muttered something that sounded like "No, Jake, no!"

Ramona moistened her handkerchief in the springwater and knelt beside Marcy while she gently bathed her face and arms. Surprisingly enough, the girl did not waken, but the muscles in her face relaxed and the creases between her eyes smoothed out. Ramona wondered whether or not Marcy was going to be able to continue at the pace Larry was setting. She would have to remind him that he was ten years older and about a hundred pounds heavier than his younger sister. If he didn't slow down, he might have one very exhausted girl to worry about.

Larry must have been reading Ramona's mind, for he rolled over on his side, propped his head on his hand, and asked, "Do you think I ought to slow down the pace, Ramona? Marcy looks really out of it. I keep forgetting that she's the youngest one of the bunch. She never complains, and she hasn't dropped very far behind yet. Do you think she suffers any aftereffects from that accident she had on the cliff a few days ago?"

"No, I don't think so," Ramona replied thoughtfully, "but I am sure that she needs some additional rest. Perhaps we can all turn in earlier this evening."

Marcy was still sleeping deeply when the rest of the group was aroused by Brig's low growls.

Larry got up suddenly and whispered, "What's wrong, Brig? Are we being invaded?"

Brig looked around at Larry and then turned back in the direction from which the party had come. By this time Kevin and Darby were up, and Brigadoon's alarm had simmered down to small muttering sounds. Kevin crept around one side of the rock, but he could see nothing. But as his glance wandered upward, he caught sight of a bearded face topped with a dark hat peering over a rock 150 yards away.

Kevin sank back against the rock, looked at the others and sighed. "It's our jinx, Jake, again! He is still on our trail. There must be some way of shaking him."

They sat around exchanging ideas about what they could do to get rid of the old man who had brought them such unpleasant times. It was Larry who finally came up with a solution to the problem. "Let's start up the trail and make an early camp. I'll tell you the rest of my plan later."

Kevin aroused Marcy, who had a hard time waking from her sleepy stupor. "How long was I conked out?" she asked with a giant yawn.

"Wow! You could win the title of Miss Grand Canyon with a yawn like that one," Darby teased. "In case you really want to know, you've been playing Rip Van Winkle for about forty-five minutes."

Marcy said nothing, but she stuck out her tongue at her cousin. The group slowly pulled themselves together to start out again on the trail.

After another hour's hiking at a somewhat slower pace, they found a small campsite among the rocks where they could bed down and not be seen by anyone unless he was almost directly above the camp. The boys scoured the area for brush and small branches for the evening's fire over which they heated some water for tea. A slim dinner of canned meat and beans helped prepare them for the night ahead. The sun quickly disappeared behind the stony cliffs, and the colors of the sky rapidly changed from orange to red and finally, as night came, to a blue-black softness against which the stars shone brightly in the Arizona sky. They all lay around the campfire with their heads on their packs, listening to the desert sounds. A lizard scurried across a rock and into the brush. A coyote howl came floating through the darkness. The embers burned low while Kevin started to talk. He spoke softly to avoid projecting his voice in the quiet stillness of the evening.

"Suppose we do find the gold mine—what will we do with all of the money?" Darby asked of no one in particular.

Larry chuckled and said, "Well, I'm not sure that I want to count my gold mines before they are discovered."

"Oh, but you must have something in mind, Larry," Darby said with a note of excitement in his voice. "Wouldn't you like to take a long trip or buy something you've always wanted?"

"I guess I would like to have a new car," Larry said thoughtfully. "The jalopy I have now just about keeps me broke buying new parts."

"I think that if I had all of the money in the world, I'd get a new color television set with a twenty-four-inch screen," said Marcy dreamily.

Darby and Kevin each thought it would be great to have two motorbikes—one for trail-riding and one for city driving. Ramona was silent. Kevin turned to her and asked, "Ramona, what would you like if we can find the mine?"

Ramona spoke very solemnly. "I will not claim a single penny of the gold, even if we do come across the mine. I believe that the gold belongs to the Apache people, who hold the treasure in trust for the gods. I have these secret fears that something evil, even worse than what has happened so far, will come our way if we keep seeking for the gold."

"Well, I don't know," Darby shot back. "So far, we have been pretty lucky."

"That's just it. So far, we *have* been lucky. But I think that the law of averages is running out and that the really bad breaks are coming our way."

Larry, sensing that an unpleasant scene might occur, suggested, "Well, I think that it is about time for all of us to turn in. We have a long day coming up."

"That's okay by me," Kevin yawned. "By the way, Larry, you haven't told us what the plan of operations is for tomorrow."

Everyone listened attentively as Larry explained. "We'll pull our bedrolls back away from the fire and behind a rock so that we can't be seen. I'll come around to each of you about an hour before dawn, just before it gets light. We'll leave the bedrolls here so that we can move out more rapidly. I hope that we can leave Jake behind. If we can get a head start and keep a decent distance between us, it may make a difference if and when we find the mine."

"Jake's no dummy," Kevin observed. "Do you really think this early rising bit will fool him?"

"I can't guarantee a thing," Larry said as he shook his head. "It's my best thought of the moment. If anyone else has a better idea, I expect that we'll all be glad to listen."

There was a long pause as everyone waited for someone to blossom forth with a better plan to insure escape from Jake's prying eyes. Everyone was tired in mind and body. The heat of the day had sapped their usually boundless energy. Eyes began to close as the fire burned itself down to quiet embers that only flared up briefly. At Larry's suggestion, the problem of Jake was put away for the more urgent matter of getting much needed sleep.

In a very short while all were dreaming of the unlimited

riches the gold would bring. All, that is, except Ramona. She waited until the sounds of deep breathing told her that the others were fast asleep. She then got up slowly and chose four twigs from the now almost empty brush pile the boys had gathered earlier. She began circling the fire ring with a slow, measured pace. When she reached the north side, she put one of the twigs on the embers. It blazed briefly into life, giving off just enough light to reveal Ramona's brown eyes shining intensely. She turned away from the fire and slowly raised her arms sideward until they were above her head. Bowing slowly and somewhat stiffly from the waist, the girl held the position for a moment and then just as slowly came erect again. This silent procedure was repeated solemnly at the east, south, and west sides.

When she had come full circle, Ramona slowly raised her arms to shoulder level and lifted her head back until her face appeared to become part of the star-studded heavens. Now she spoke softly.

"Spirits of my Apache ancestors, hear my words. Forgive these people their invasion of our spiritual home. Their greed for gold overcomes their other, better selves. I cannot convince them that they will not win out in their efforts to wrestle our treasure from us. Even though they are blinded by their search for gold, they are still my friends, and I beg you to protect them from harm while they pass through these mountains. Send them a sign, a thunderous sign of your displeasure, one they cannot ignore. But let them return home safely."

Ramona lowered her arms and her head slowly and stood for a long time in deep thought. In the dim and flickering light the prayerful figure was only a small shadow lost in the immense Arizona night. Would the Apache gods hear her words?

Early the next morning, in the weak light shed by a splinter of a moon, Larry made the rounds to each bedroll and quietly whispered in each sleeper's ear. "Get up quietly. We're moving out in five minutes."

Surprisingly enough, not a sound came from anyone as, keenly aware that they had to get rid of the old man, they all quietly became part of the shadowy night and moved along the trail. Each kept in touch with the other by a piece of rope tied around his waist and fastened to the person behind. Larry was in the lead with a small flashlight covered with paper. Only a tiny hole let out enough light to avoid bushes and boulders in the path. Even Brig was preoccupied with the path, so that he didn't sense what was happening behind him.

Not far to the rear of the hikers was a much older and grimmer figure who quietly stalked along, keeping a wary ear attuned to the progress of the party ahead. The head of the man was covered with a battered hat, and the face was half hidden behind a long, untidy beard.

15

THROUGH THE LOOKING GLASS

After they had been traveling for about an hour, the sun rose slowly, and rock formations that had been ghostly gargoyles took on more friendly faces. Sounds that, when it was dark, the young people had variously interpreted as rattlesnakes slithering along the ground or coyotes stalking them, were now seen to be nothing more than noises made by dislodged rocks or perhaps the hum of the wind through paloverde trees.

As they were able to see more, Larry found it less necessary to put miles between them and whatever lay behind.

"Okay, gang," he said. "Let's stop for a rest and untie ourselves. I don't think we'll need that rope for a while."

"Good," said Marcy grouchily. "Between Darby in front of me and Ramona behind me, I thought I was gonna be pulled apart." After removing the rope, she sank wearily to the ground.

"You are tired, aren't you, Little One?" said Ramona gently, pushing the hair out of Marcy's eyes. "Try to get some rest now."

"Let's have something to eat," urged Kevin. "If Jake were behind us, we could see him. We don't have to be so careful now. Besides, I'm starved."

Ramona looked through each person's backpack in order to decide how much they could afford to eat. "I don't think we'd better start a fire," she advised. "So whatever we have, we'll have to eat cold."

"Fine with me," said Darby, "as long as it's food."

Ramona opened a can of meat and a can of beans and carefully doled some out to each person, giving Marcy an extra spoonful of beans after the others had been served.

"We don't have much farther to go to get into the position we want," said Larry, surveying the country around them. "Saddle Bluffs is over there."

He pointed to a rock formation that was visible to them for the first time. It was some distance away, and could be glimpsed only through the space between two other rock formations. Yet its unique shape, two high rounded rock bluffs with a low, almost flat area in between did indeed suggest a saddle.

As Darby caught sight of the formation, he felt his pulse leaping in spite of himself. Could that be where the fabulous Lost Dutchman Mine was really located, and were they to be the ones who would actually discover the great treasure?

"If we find the mine and get out of here, we may never need to eat beans again," said Darby, "but I must say that right at the moment they taste as good as anything that I can imagine. And the canned meat isn't half bad either."

"You said a mouthful," said Kevin. He turned to his brother. "What's our next move, Larry? It shouldn't take us more than half an hour to get to Saddle Bluffs and that will be too early to see if our theory about the map is correct."

"Yes," said Marcy, her mouth full of food. "What are we

gonna do to kill time? I sure don't want to sit around in this heat."

"I don't blame you, Sis," answered Larry. "I don't think any of us do. As much prospecting as there has been in this area, there should be lots of tunnels. What do you say we find one that's located up high enough so that we can keep an eye on the trail and keep cool at the same time? Before we start looking for the mine, I want to be darned sure that we have gotten rid of that crazy Dutchman."

"You and me both," said Marcy. "I sure don't want to run into him again like I did that first time. Especially now that I know what a nutty old coot he really is."

"Okay, then," said Larry. "As soon as you all feel that you've had plenty of rest, let's get loaded up and move on. I don't want to rush you, but the sooner we move, the sooner we can find a cool place."

The five adventurers were soon headed in the direction of Saddle Bluffs. No longer tied together by the rope, Marcy, Kevin, and Darby became playful, challenging one another to various dares in an impromptu game of Follow the Leader.

When the three youngest members of the party had gotten several yards ahead on the trail, Ramona, who had been bringing up the rear, hurried to catch up with Larry.

"You don't really think we've lost Jake, do you?" she asked calmly.

"For the time being I think we have," answered Larry. "He's an old man and we've been moving right along."

"He's a clever old man, too," countered Ramona with quiet emphasis. "He's crazy like a fox. Don't forget he's been out here in the Superstitions a long time. He's learned how to survive. And he's learned how to track."

"I know," Larry answered, "but I think we've outfoxed him this time by getting up early. You haven't seen any sign of him, have you?"

"Not yet," said Ramona. "But that doesn't mean much out here. We're not too hard to follow, and there are hundreds of places for him to hide."

"I realize that," said Larry, speaking a little sharply. "That's why we're going to hide for a while. If he is after us, we can see him and he won't be able to see us."

"I know that you think you are being careful, and I can understand your wish to find the mine," answered Ramona, "but I want to appeal to you one more time to give up your search. Look at what has happened to nearly everyone who has tried to find it. There is a reason for that. With your college education, you think, I know, that my Apache beliefs are a bunch of nonsense, but the facts prove otherwise."

"Ramona, there has been a logical explanation for every death that has ever occurred here in the mountains," said Larry.

"Do you call men's lust for gold a logical reason for killing?" asked the Indian girl.

"Not logical, perhaps," Larry replied, "but we at least know that these people weren't killed by ghosts or by the lost tribes of Montezuma."

"The method doesn't matter," Ramona answered calmly. "The fact is that the Apache gods are keeping watch over this area. The gold is theirs, and they guard it jealously. I truly believe the map you have found will lead you to the treasure, but I also believe that it may mean your death."

A look of deep concern crossed Larry's face and he turned to the solemn girl.

"I mean no disrespect for your religion, Ramona, but I simply cannot believe the way you do. The gold is here for the taking, just as it was at Sutter's Mill or at the Vulture Mine near Wickenburg."

"I see that I cannot convince you about the sanctity of this place, so I must try to appeal to you another way," said

Ramona, looking deeply into Larry's eyes.

Larry did not answer, but waited for her to continue.

"You have the map," she said. "You can come back another time. You and I have been given the care of Marcy and Kevin and Darby. Even if there is just a small chance that I am right, I don't think that you should expose those three kids to any more danger. We know that Jake means business. He's tried to kill us before."

"I don't doubt that he stole your food," answered Larry, "but I don't know about the rock that fell on the line shack. He could have accidentally dislodged it. I mean, what would he have to gain by killing anyone?"

"I tell you the man is loco," replied Ramona, becoming impatient. "We can't begin to know what a mind like his is thinking. By now he probably believes that he is the Dutchman himself and that these mountains belong to him. There is no telling what he might do. And there are other dangers. Let's get out of here and get the kids to safety. We owe it to your parents to take care of them."

Larry smiled reassuringly at Ramona. "I know that you are sincere," he said. "But I don't share your concern. After we get rid of Jake today, all we have to do is see if the map is right. Then we'll head out of here. I can't deprive the kids of the chance to be in on that discovery. You know how disappointed Darby would be if he had to go home now. Give him a chance to think that the West can be the way he always thought it should be. We'll go home tomorrow."

Their conversation was interrupted by Marcy, who came running back.

"Come on, you all," she shouted. "Kevin's found the perfect cave or tunnel or whatever it is. It's up behind a rock and it's dark and cool and we can watch the trail from there. We've already checked it out. Come on!"

Larry looked at Ramona apologetically and shrugged his

shoulders. Marcy grabbed Ramona's hand, and the three of them hurried up the trail to join the two boys.

Kevin's discovery turned out to be a cave, and it was everything Marcy had said and more. It had a narrow entrance that was partially hidden by a tall rock that stood about two feet in front of it. The inside was roomy and was cooled by a small spring that dropped from the roof of the cavern. To Larry's delight there were petroglyphs on the wall. As he set up his camera to photograph them, Ramona stood at the door, keeping watch on the trail below.

Nearly an hour had passed happily in the comfort of the cave when Ramona rose from her seat near the entrance and placed her finger to her lips.

Marcy saw the signal and spoke to the boys. "Quiet, you guys, I think Ramona sees something."

All talk ceased as they gathered near Ramona and peered at a spot below on the trail. What they saw was a very red-faced Jake moving rapidly along the trail, stopping only occasionally to scan the surrounding area through a pair of binoculars.

"Get back," whispered Ramona. "He may look up here at any minute."

As the others stepped back, Ramona continued to watch.

"Is he still looking around?" asked Marcy.

"No, he's starting to move," answered Ramona. As Jake passed below them and headed toward Saddle Bluffs, the others stood and watched. Finally he passed between the twin cliffs and was lost from sight.

"I think we've gotten rid of him now for sure," said Larry. "Pretty soon now we can go see if our theory about the map is correct."

"How's it gonna work?" asked Darby.

"Well," Larry replied, "we'll spread out along the side of the bluffs and find the spot where we can see the sun on the very top of Weaver's Needle at four o'clock. Then we'll see if there is a Y formation someplace near. If we find a Y formation, like two arroyos coming together to form one ravine or something like that, we'll look for some sign of a tunnel around there."

A little before four o'clock they were moving slowly up and down the bluffs, watching for the place where the sun appeared to rest on the formation known as Weaver's Needle. Ramona did not join in the search, but she did watch the trail for any sign of Jake.

It was Larry who finally saw the sun come into position and quickly marked the spot as the others ran to join him.

"Spread out around here," commanded Larry, "and look for something that looks like a Y formation."

Back and forth they walked, but there was nothing that even their fertile imaginations could construe as resembling a Y.

"Let's spread out over the entire side of the bluff," said Larry. "Maybe four o'clock when the map was made was different from four o'clock now. Let's form a line and move all along this area. Remember, we're looking for some sort of Y formation."

For the next two hours all of them, with the exception of Ramona, moved along the slope of the bluffs, stopping at any mark in the terrain that might suggest a Y. First one and then another shouted for Larry to come and look at something they had discovered. But Larry was never convinced that they had found any clue of significance. Finally, tired and disappointed, they sat down for a consultation.

"Either the map is a phony or we've figured it wrong," said Kevin.

"You're right," Darby agreed. "Or maybe someone put some extra symbols on the map to fool people. I've heard there are some characters who do that sort of thing."

Kevin blushed and the others laughed as they remembered the alterations Kevin had made on Larry's map.

"And maybe if we'd hold it up to a mirror, we could figure it out," Darby added, laughing again at Kevin's discomfort.

"What's this about a mirror?" asked Larry.

"Kevin said that sometimes they used to make maps backward so that you had to hold them up to a mirror to read them," Darby told him.

Larry didn't laugh as Darby expected, but, instead, he spread the map on the ground.

"I thought something didn't look quite right about this map," he said. "It *is* drawn backward. Look at the way Weaver's Needle is sketched. See this bulge right here in the needle? Now look at Weaver's Needle on the ground. See? The bulge is on the other side. We've been looking on the wrong side of Saddle Bluff. The mine is on the other horn of the saddle. I just know it is. It's getting late now, but tomorrow we'll find it."

Larry stood up and folded the map. "We'll get some rest now and get up early and look for the mine," he told them. "Maybe we won't have to actually see where the sun will be at four o'clock. We can calculate ahead and concentrate our search in that area."

"I don't know if you've noticed," put in Ramona, "but we're nearly out of food, and it's going to take us a couple of days to get back to the jeep."

"We can get more food at the line shack, can't we?" asked Darby.

"We're taking a chance," said Ramona. "For all we know, someone who came along after us may have taken the food. We just can't depend on finding anything to eat there."

"I don't mind being a little hungry if we're going to get rich," said Darby.

"You may get more than just a little hungry," replied

Ramona. "I should think you'd remember how close we came to dying on the way up. This place is a killer, and death from hunger or thirst can be pretty horrible. I really think that we should start back without delay."

"Just a couple of hours to search tomorrow and then we'll head home," Kevin promised sincerely.

"There's another thing you're forgetting," Ramona added. "Your parents are due back soon. They will be panic-stricken if they get home and we're not there, even if they do find our note."

"Two hours in the morning to look for the mine and then we'll start home. I promise," said Larry, holding up his hand. "Honest Injun."

Ramona sighed and smiled weakly. "What can one redskin do against four white eyes?" she asked. "Come on, let's see what we have to eat."

Later, as the last rays of the sun illuminated the top of Weaver's Needle, first one and then another began to yawn. "We'll turn in early tonight so we can get an early start," said Larry.

"Fine with me," answered Darby. "I'm beat."

"Don't get too comfy yet," said Ramona quietly. "We may be moving out soon." Saying this, she pointed toward the crest of Saddle Bluffs. Marcy's eyes followed where Ramona's arm pointed and she stifled a scream. Silhouetted against the red sky stood two figures, a pack-laden burro and Jake, a shotgun resting across his arm.

16

BRIG DROPS OUT OF SIGHT

"Get down, everybody," Kevin shouted as the group scattered, ducking behind various boulders.

"I thought we were rid of him," said Darby. "I wonder if he's been watching us all day."

Ramona squatted by Marcy, who was whimpering quietly. "He's never gonna leave us alone," sobbed Marcy. "Let's go home. I'm tired of this awful place."

"It'll be dark in an hour or so," said Larry quietly. "Then we're moving out. Keep your chin up, Marcy. I won't let anything happen to you. We're going to go around to the other side of the bluff and find a place to hide. That way we'll be in a position to start the search early. Then we're heading home."

Nearly three hours later, scratched by cacti, bruised by rocks, and tired and thirsty, the five explorers came to a halt on the opposite side of Saddle Bluffs. Larry had led them by moonlight to a narrow ravine that pierced the bluff.

"I think we'll be safe here," said Larry wearily. "At least we can't be seen from three sides. We can take turns keeping watch for Jake in case he's still following us. I'll take the first shift while the rest of you turn in."

When the first rays of the morning sun hit the campsite, Larry, who was slumped against a rock, awoke. He had fallen asleep on the first shift of the watch and had slept all through the night as had the other tired hikers. Feeling a bit sheepish, Larry yawned, stretched, and then wakened the others.

"I'm afraid I let you down," he explained to them. "I fell asleep on guard duty, but I guess it's all right. Brig didn't bark, and I haven't seen any sign of Jake."

"Boy! We could have woke up dead," said Marcy, hitting her older brother playfully on the arm as everyone joined in with hoots and laughter.

"Sorry about that," said Larry. "What do you say we skip breakfast and start our search now. Maybe we can be gone before Jake is even awake."

"Okay," said Kevin, rubbing his eyes, "but let's get our bearings. We've got to find a place as far up on this side of the Bluffs as we were yesterday at four o'clock on the other side. I remember seeing that rock up there from the other bluff. It sort of looks like a face. The mine should be located about halfway between that spot and the top of the saddle. At least that's my guess."

Arriving at the area Kevin had shown them, Marcy, Larry, Darby, and Kevin fanned out. Back and forth they paced, looking for something that resembled the letter Y. For nearly an hour they searched, covering a wider and wider area.

"Looks like we're stymied again," shouted Darby. "We must be doing something wrong." Wearily he sat down on the edge of a cleft rock, where he was joined by Marcy.

"Boy, I'm bushed," she said, taking a drink from her canteen. She sat down on a small rock and looked up at Darby, who was perched above her. They were soon joined by Kevin. He appeared tired and defeated.

"I give up," he said. "I haven't seen anything that has the vaguest resemblance to a Y."

They sat silently, waiting for Larry to join them. After looking up at the two boys sitting above her, Marcy examined the rock on which she was perched. "I wonder if this rock broke off from the one you're sitting on," she pondered.

"What difference does it make?" asked Darby impatiently.

"Well," Marcy answered, "if it did break off that rock, would the formation have looked like a Y before?"

Kevin jumped down from his perch and looked at the two rocks. "You may just be right," he said to his sister, becoming more and more excited as he looked from one rock to the other. "Hey, Darb, come here and have a look!"

"See," said Marcy, "if this rock were put up where that cracked place is, wouldn't that be sort of a Y?"

Just as they were ready to shout to Larry, they heard a dog's bark, seemingly coming from far away.

"Where's Brig?" asked Marcy. "He was digging by that bunch of rocks down the slope there just a few minutes ago. Here, Brig!" she called.

Again they heard his bark but were unable to pinpoint his location.

"I'm going to look for him," said Kevin, starting down the slope below them. As he carefully let himself down the steep bank, he heard Brig's bark again, and, almost simultaneously, he noticed a hole in the ground. Dropping to his knees, he peered into the opening. With his hands, he began to enlarge the hole, and a boulder broke loose as he dug.

Again he heard Brig's bark, and this time he knew that the curious little terrier was in the hole. Darby joined Kevin, and the two of them began pulling boulders away from around the opening, making it about a yard wide.

As they stood back to catch their breaths, Brig came bounding out of the hole.

"You know," said Darby excitedly, "I think the Lost Dutchman Mine has just been discovered by a dog."

"Larry," Marcy shouted. "Come quick! We've found it! We've found the mine!"

As they waited for Larry, Darby and Kevin peered into the cavern, which extended straight back into the side of the hill. Because they could not see any supporting timbers, it was difficult to tell whether or not the hole in the earth was a mine.

"What do you think?" asked Kevin as Larry joined them. "Is it really a mine?"

Larry shone his flashlight back into the hole. "I think it is," he answered, his voice quavering with emotion. "We'll have to be careful, but I think we can go in safely."

The three boys began to clear more boulders from the entry as Brig barked his approval. When they had cleared a large opening and no more debris fell from above, Larry spoke. "Okay, get your flashlights and let's go. Take it slow and be ready to run back out if we have to."

As the three boys entered the cavern, Ramona stood holding Marcy's hand.

"Come on, Ramona," said Marcy, pulling on Ramona's arm. "I don't want to miss out on the excitement."

As though in a daze, Ramona allowed herself to be led into the mine that had opened almost mysteriously in the side of the hill.

17

LIGHT AT THE END OF THE TUNNEL

Stepping even a few paces inside the tunnel brought a welcome change from the stifling heat on the mountainside. The coolness of the mine bathed sweaty faces and brought an immediate sigh of relief from Darby, who expressed everyone's feelings when he said, "Whew! I don't know how safe this place is, but it sure is great to beat the heat. It must be thirty degrees cooler in here."

Kevin made himself immediately popular when he suggested that they leave their packs along the side of the mine and pick them up on the way out later on.

"Good idea, Kev," said Larry. "We'll only need our flashlights, canteens, and some extra batteries. I'm on my last three now. Kevin, be sure to bring that rope you've been carrying in case we find another down shaft."

With the loads off their backs, everyone took the opportunity to stretch a bit. It was Larry who noticed that this mine was different from the other they had explored.

"Hey, gang, did you notice that I can stretch and not touch the roof?"

"Yeah," said Marcy, "and it seems to be quite a bit wider, too."

Larry added, "I've been looking at the ruts in the floor. I would guess that a lot of rock was unloaded from these diggings. This mine was evidently so large that they needed a wagon or cart to move the ore outside."

Darby spoke thoughtfully. "I'm wondering if this could have been the chief source of Peralta's gold?"

"Well, maybe we can find out. We ought to get started exploring the rest of the mine," Kevin urged.

As the party moved along, they discovered that the diggers of this mine had taken more care in its construction than in the one they had explored earlier. Every ten feet or so, poles cut from trees supported bigger poles that stretched across the ceiling. Some of these supports, as well as those along the sides of the mine, were missing, and many others appeared to be rotten. Once in a while, dirt and small rocks showered down on the hikers, making them splutter and pause to wipe the sand and dust from their eyes.

It was Marcy who let out a small cry as she shone her light into a small crypt on the side.

"Wow, look at this!" she exclaimed.

"Don't tell us you've found another skeleton," Darby said, pretending to appear just a bit bored. "One of those a day keeps hikers away." Darby sounded flippant, but it was just his way of showing how tired and nervous he had become in the past few days.

"No, I'm serious," Marcy replied.

"Well, how do you do, Serious," Darby quipped again, with a giggle.

"Let's see what Marcy has discovered," Larry said, somewhat impatient with Darby's attempt at being funny. While the others crowded around, Larry stooped over and carefully picked up some shreds of material from which dangled a large metal object.

"It looks man-made," said Marcy. "Maybe it's a strap with a buckle attached."

It was indeed a buckle about three inches long and two inches wide and oval in shape. There was a smaller opening in the center behind which were two stout metal rods spaced about half an inch apart. The remains of a leather strap were laced through these rods, cinching the strap tightly in place. Larry rubbed the buckle on the sole of his shoe to remove as much grime and corrosion as possible. When this didn't produce satisfactory results, he carried the object to the wall, and in a few seconds the bright metal shone through.

"Look, it's silver!" he exclaimed. "It looks sturdy enough to have been on a pack or maybe a saddlebag. Here's something interesting! A crown has been stamped on the edge."

"Which means that it must have been made in a country ruled by a king or queen," Darby observed.

"I'd say it is a Spanish or Mexican piece," said Larry thoughtfully. "If I recall the story correctly, the Apaches, after they had done away with Peralta and his men, returned some of the bags of gold to the mines. We are probably looking at the remains of one of those old Spanish saddlebags."

Larry suddenly dropped again to his knees and began scrabbling about in the small rocks near the place where the buckle was found. He snatched up a few of the dirty looking chunks, spit on them, and rubbed them on his pant leg.

"Everybody concentrate your light on the rock I'm holding," he ordered.

The hands holding the lights shook a bit from excitement and fatigue, but the combined beams were bright enough for Larry to see flecks of a yellow mineral. His face broke into a wide grin. He threw back his head and laughed so strangely that the others thought he must have suffered from overexposure to the sun.

"Okay, Larry," said Kevin impatiently. "What's so funny?"

"Sorry, gang. I'm laughing because I'm relieved and partly because I can't believe that we have stumbled on what actually seems to be one of the Peralta mines. This mine could be the most important one of all!"

There was immediate bedlam as everyone except Ramona quickly dropped to his knees and began digging through the rocks. Kevin was the first to pause and say to Larry, "What do you think the ore is worth?"

"I'd guess that this sample would assay out at about a hundred ounces to the ton. And that's a bonanza in anybody's language!"

Darby's mind raced ahead. "How will we get the gold out of here? It's a whale of a long way to just about any place. It is going to cost a lot of money just to get equipment up here to enlarge the mine and dig the ore."

Ramona answered Darby in a voice with a slight quiver. If the others had been looking closely, they would have seen her usual calm was on the verge of breaking down. The hardships of hiking for many days were beginning to tell, for her round face looked pinched and haggard. But more than that, the constant tension of sharing her loyalties between her friends and her gods was beginning to show in the shortness of her temper.

"Darby, many people have paid a very high cost for the privilege of searching for this treasure. Some have lost fortunes. Others have been wounded, and not a few have paid the greatest cost of all, their lives."

Ramona's serious demeanor once again dropped a cloud of gloom over the party, but her speech was not enough to make them abandon their search. They had caught the yellow mineral disease, and everything they saw was colored gold. They just couldn't turn back now! There were probably greater treasures just ahead. Everyone except Ramona returned to stuffing his pockets with the nuggets until Larry brought them up short with a sharp tone in his voice.

"Just a cotton-picking minute! Why carry these rocks farther into the mine and then back out again? Let's leave my bandanna as a marker. On the way back, we'll load up our packs with as much as we can carry."

"I think I'll keep mine over here," said Kevin, starting to stack his nuggets apart from the others.

"Just as I thought," murmured Ramona half aloud. "Already the gold is starting to have its effect on you. Kevin wants his own pile, and he'll be watching to see that no one else gets more than he does."

This rather startling change in Kevin brought everyone to a halt. They turned and watched him curiously. Kevin stopped, looked around, held his rocks close to his chest for a moment, and then broke into a sheepish grin.

"I'm sorry," he said sincerely. "I completely forgot myself. With us, it's one for all and all for one." He quickly brought his nuggets back to the common pile and dumped them with the others.

The hikers then picked up their flashlights and moved off down the mine corridor. Farther along, Larry stopped and shone his light to the right. The beam traveled for twenty-five yards or so and then struck what looked like a wall. His curiosity was aroused. "Let's see where this leads us," he said, leading the way into the opening.

The side shaft quickly became smaller and narrower until each hiker had to squat and waddle along in duck fashion as he passed through a narrow opening which then expanded into a small room, with barely enough room to stand upright.

When everybody was inside, Marcy, noticing how

crowded it was, said with a small quaver in her voice, "I sure wouldn't like to stay in here very long. Without lights it would be awful. What was the point in digging off the main tunnel and then stopping?"

"Probably a vein of gold ran off in this direction, and the miners just followed it until it ran out. The vein possibly branched out where this room is, and the room was formed as the ore was hauled away," Kevin said.

Larry had been busy searching the walls and ceiling of the room with his flashlight beam. "The rock is quite different in here than in the main tunnel," he said. "It is softer. Did you notice where they tried to shore up the ceiling so that it wouldn't fall?"

"There's not too much left of the timbers now," Darby said uneasily. "In fact, it doesn't really look safe in here. I'm beginning to wonder if we should be in here at all."

Ramona spoke again. "I noticed that the outside entrance was also beginning to sag. The entire mine is about as unsafe as any I've seen."

Larry spoke rather swiftly. "Well, let's not tempt fate. We'd better get out while the getting's good. There doesn't appear to be any valuable ore in this room anyway."

The party made its way back to the main gallery where the hikers were soon stopped by the end wall of the mine. There, a small, steep slope led up to a ledge which was dug back into the rock for about five to ten feet.

Larry said, "Shine your lights up there, while I claw my way up and see what we have."

All lights swung almost in unison onto the ledge. After Larry made it to the top, he wiggled his way back into the depths of the ledge where he lay on his side so that he could better chip away at the wall with a chunk of ore.

"The rock seems to have a slight pinkish color," Marcy said.

Larry grunted, "It's pink quartz mixed in with some other minerals."

Darby wasn't patient enough to just stand and hold a light for Larry. He propped his lamp so that it shone on Larry's area while he began pecking away at the wall to his left. He was wielding a fairly large rock that just barely fit into his fist. A flurry of blows against the side of the shaft brought down some large pebbles and a great deal of dust from the ceiling.

"Careful, Darb," Kevin warned. "The roof in here doesn't look too secure."

Darby's taste for gold had grown into a man-sized hunger that made him disregard any possible danger. After one particularly hard blow, an odd shaped chunk of rock seemed to leap from the side of the mine and tumbled to the floor. Darby bent down, picked it up, and rubbed off the dirt. When the nugget gleamed brightly, Darby let out a yell and rushed over to the others. He was so excited that even Larry scrambled down to find out what the hubbub was all about.

After squinting at Darby's find for a moment, he gave a long, low whistle. "Darby, old man, you lucky son of a gun! You are holding in your hand a nugget that must be worth at least a couple hundred dollars! It seems to be almost entirely virgin gold."

"Wow," whispered Darby. "That's about one tenth of the cost of my first motorcycle."

Larry gave Darby back his nugget, put his hands on his hips and announced in a quiet tone that barely concealed the excitement in his voice. "It looks as if we may have discovered the mother lode mine from which Peralta hauled most of his gold."

"The mother lode?" said Marcy. "I don't understand."

"Well," explained Larry, "when gold is formed, there is usually a main pool from which the smaller veins form. The main source is called the mother lode by miners. It contains most of the gold and is the part of the deposit all the miners hope they will find. This could be the one that Peralta discovered the second year he dug in this area. We can be pretty sure that this is the mine that old Jacob Walz drew on the map we followed."

The young people had formed a small semicircle around Larry with their backs to the entrance of the mine. All the lights were shining on him and the gold he held in his hands. Suddenly Brigadoon perked up his ears, sprang off his haunches, and dashed a few feet in the direction of the entrance to the mine. He skidded to a halt, barking shrilly all the time. Immediately all conversation ceased.

Larry whispered urgently, "Put out your lights! Move to each side of the mine and squat down on the floor."

Everybody huddled quietly in the inky blackness, not knowing what to expect next. Only the soft sifting of bits of rock from the mine ceiling could be heard.

Abruptly the darkness was pierced with a bright beam of light that made its blinding round from one startled face to another. While Brig stood his ground and growled as fiercely as he could, the bearded man with a battered hat threw back his head and cackled almost insanely. The barrel of the shotgun in his hand glittered in the lamplight. He waved the weapon several times in front of the hikers who were huddled on the floor, and finally spoke.

"Vell, vell! We finally meet again. You have been trying to escape me for days. But ol' Jake is too clever for you. You haven't been out of my sight, not since you left the little cabin. How can I ever thank you enough for finding my grandfather's mine?"

18

THUNDER IN THE SUPERSTITIONS

The sudden appearance of Jake, with his scraggly beard, his crazy laugh, and the shotgun which he brandished so nervously, had a demoralizing effect. The rugged hiking and the tension caused by the "accidents" had worn their stamina and control to the breaking point. The uncertainty of what was going to happen to them temporarily broke their spirits. Marcy broke into uncontrollable sobs.

"Oh, Larry, what are we going to do? How are we ever going to get out of this mess?"

Larry, who for a short time had been stunned by the sudden turn of events, quickly regained his presence of mind. In a low voice he whispered to Marcy, "Come on, Sis, pull yourself together. We'll come out of this smelling like a rose."

Jake, unfortunately, overheard what Larry said. "So, you think that you will get out of this alive, eh? What a dreamer you are! I have been searching for a long time for my grandfather's treasure. I have been searching for months for this mine. I will not have it stolen from under my nose by a group of young brats."

By this time Kevin had regained some of his usual spunk. "Okay, old man, you hold the gun. What's next?"

"You will find out soon enough," Jake growled.

Ramona slowly rose to her feet and spoke. As she did so, Jake's light swung to her face, which reflected a proud serenity, making her truly beautiful despite the grime accumulated over the past days. She spoke slowly and with dignity.

"White man, you know that I am an Apache Indian. You may not know that my gods inhabit these mountains and that my people consider these lands sacred. Our Thunder Gods have always spoken in the loudest tones, and men have listened or suffered the consequences. Do you think that where others have failed you can succeed? It will go better with you if you leave our treasure and let us go our way in peace."

Jake turned on her viciously and shouted, jabbing with the gun for emphasis. "Your treasure? The gold rightfully belongs to me. What kind of fool do you take me for that I should let you go back to your people and to the police?"

Darby, who had been quiet up to now, spoke out in a loud voice. "Okay, Jake, if you don't care enough to honor Ramona's religion, then you had better believe that Kevin's family are probably out hunting for us now. Whatever you do will be found out and you'll have to pay the penalty, especially if we don't come back alive."

Jake laughed scornfully. "Well, we will just have to see about that when the time comes." Pointing to Kevin, he ordered, "Take off that rope and put it at your feet." Kevin hastily removed the rope he had used to rappel down Apache Leap and gingerly laid it in front of his shoes.

"All the rest of you," Jake commanded, "empty your pockets and put what you have at your feet." When he saw that the younger boys had knives, he jabbed his light in the direction of Kevin and commanded, "You, unwrap that rope and cut off pieces about three feet long. Hurry!" In just a few minutes Kevin had slashed the rope into several lengths. He put the knife back on the floor and looked up for further instructions.

Jake's attention, however, had turned to Ramona. "You, Indian girl, start tying hands behind the back. Begin with the big one over there. Tie good knots. I'll be watching carefully."

Ramona picked up a piece of rope and started to bind Larry's wrists. Larry turned his head slightly and looked intently at the girl as though he was trying to tell her something. Ramona caught his glance, although she didn't fully understand until she noticed that the muscles in Larry's wrists were tense and rigid. Then she knew that he was trying to keep his muscles as large as possible so that when she finished he would relax and there would be room to slip his hands free. But Jake was aware of the rope trick. He called Larry over, ordered him to lie down on his stomach while he tested the tightness of the knots. Cursing loudly, Jake made the girl retie the knots.

Marcy was the last to be bound. Before starting, Ramona turned to the old man and requested softly, "Look how upset this poor girl is. Does she have to be bound also?"

Jake was unmoved. "Everybody gets bound. Quickly!"

By this time Marcy had cried herself dry and was slowly regaining her composure.

"Ramona," she said bravely, "I want to go along with the others. I want to be with you."

Ramona replied soothingly. "You are a brave girl, Marcy. I love you as a sister, and of course we'll stay together."

When the last knot was tied, Jake commanded, "Follow me. Do not try anything, anything at all. I will not hesitate to shoot." He meant every word, and all five obediently followed him as he backed up along the mine corridor, keeping his light moving between the path ahead and the captives behind. When he came to the narrow passageway that led to the small room, he herded the group in that direction.

"You, Larry, go in first," Jake said gruffly. "Indian girl, you will go in last. The others, follow the big one. When you get into the room, lie on the floor, facedown. And not a single false move from anyone."

When the others had stumbled their way into the cramped space, Ramona turned to Jake and looked him in the eye calmly. "What do you want me to do?"

"Take this extra rope, go inside, and tie each person's legs together. No more tricks. Tie them tightly."

Ramona did as she was told, and then crawled out through the entryway and stood before her captor. "Now what?" she asked.

"Lie facedown on the ground with your hands behind your back," Jake snarled. Ramona complied, and although Jake bound her hands so tightly that she winced in pain, she kept silent. The German then ordered her into the room with the others. He shone his light into the room and said with a crooked smile, "You are all being good boys and girls. Stay that way. If I hear the slightest sound, I shall fire into the room."

Jake propped his light so that it shone partly on the entrance to the room and partly inside. He took Larry's flashlight and moved off into the darkness. His footsteps could be heard going in the direction of the face of the mine. It was Darby who whispered, "Larry, what can we do?"

Larry turned his head and spoke in Darby's direction. "I don't know yet. Be still for a while and let's see what the old goat has on his mind. We can't do much with our hands and feet tied. I was hoping that he wouldn't check on how tight you tied my hands, Ramona."

"I know," she replied wistfully. "He's a crafty old devil.

We will have to be careful of what we do."

"What do you think he's going to do?" asked Marcy, her voice trembling.

"I don't know," said Larry thoughtfully. "I'm pretty sure, though, that he'll be back soon. Quiet! Here he comes."

Jake appeared with his shotgun slung over his shoulder. In his arms were two large rocks, which he deposited in front of the small entryway.

"What's he up to?" Darby asked.

"That stinking old man plans to block up the entrance and leave us here," Larry responded angrily.

Jake had overheard Larry's bitter comment, and he responded by laughing cruelly and commenting as he stomped off into the darkness, "You have finally caught on to the plan, boy."

This news sent Marcy back into hysterics. "I'm sorry," she sobbed, "but I just can't stand to think that I'll never see daylight or Mom again."

Darby had a lump in his throat, and when he tried to soothe Marcy, he wasn't up to the task. He started to tell her not to worry, but his voice cracked, and he kept silent while tears rolled down his cheeks.

"Oh, come on, guys and gals," said Larry, feeling sorry that he had spoken so plainly. "This isn't going to help a bit. We've got to do some clear thinking and stop feeling sorry for ourselves. I have an idea that might work. Where is Brigadoon?"

Upon hearing his name, the terrier crawled to Larry and licked his cheek.

"Brig, stay by me, and when Jake comes back and I give the word, you go get him!" Larry knew that Brigadoon didn't understand, even though the little dog whimpered a bit. More than anything, Larry wanted to practice a plan in his mind and give a little encouragement to the others.

Jake returned with a second load of rocks, bigger than those he had before. He dropped them with a thud and a grunt, glad to be free of his burden. Because the shotgun kept slipping off his shoulder, the German leaned his weapon against the wall. Larry, who had rolled into a position on his side, turned his head so that he could watch Jake.

Just as the old man stooped over to lift a rock, Larry gave Brigadoon a firm command, "Get 'im, Brig, get 'im!"

Brig shot toward the entrance like a hunting dog about to close in on its prey. Taking a mighty leap, the tiny terrier cleared the rock barricade and sank his sharp teeth into his victim's wrist. Jake screamed in surprise as much as pain, and threw his arm back over his head. Midway in flight, the dog lost his grip and crashed to the floor where he lay whimpering softly.

As Jake fell backward, he groped for something to check his fall. His free hand came in contact with the top of the shotgun and slid down the barrel onto the trigger guard. Unable to control his fall, Jake's fingers yanked both triggers, setting off two deafening explosions that echoed throughout the mine for several seconds. The shells blasted a large hole in the roof, which started to crumble. One rock about the size of a football crashed into Jake's skull. The bearded man's scream of pain could be heard throughout the mine. He lost consciousness quickly and lay silent, with only an occasional spastic jerk to indicate that he was still alive.

In a few minutes the dust had settled somewhat. Many pieces of the roof continued to fall around the entryway, which was slowly being closed.

Larry quickly checked with the others. "Everybody all right?"

After everyone had responded, Larry spoke to Ramona. "Wiggle over this way and lie with your back to mine. That's right. Now, slip your hand into my right pocket. You'll find a penknife there. I didn't give it up when Jake ordered us to. A little farther down. Good girl! Now see if you can open the blade and hold the knife steady. I want you to help me cut the rope."

Larry twisted his body until he felt the knife blade between his fingers. Very carefully, he lowered his arms until the blade was on the rope. By moving his hands back and forth for about five minutes, he was able to free his arms.

"Wonderful! I was beginning to think that I didn't have hands. I wonder what happened to Jake?"

"I don't know," responded Kevin. "I'm more interested in what happened to Brigadoon. Brig, are you out there?"

The dog whimpered a little and barked weakly, but he didn't join the others. Kevin cried, "I know he's been hurt. Hold on, Brig, we're coming."

"Take it easy, Kevin. Brig is probably okay," said Darby. "We'll go take a look at him as soon as we get free of these ropes. Larry, are you going to cut us loose?"

"Yeah, I sure am. Be right there."

In a few minutes they were all rubbing their wrists and ankles and preparing to move out of the mine. Larry, the first to bend over Jake's body, saw that there was a nasty bruise on the old man's head and that he was bleeding from the mouth and nose. Larry stooped and put his ear on Jake's chest to listen for a heartbeat.

"He's still alive, but I think he needs a doctor badly. We had better get him and ourselves out of here while we can. This mine looks as though it will cave in any minute."

Kevin and Marcy had gone to examine Brigadoon, who lay looking up at them with sad eyes. He tried to stand, but his right rear leg was evidently broken.

Marcy dropped to her knees and sobbed, "Oh, Brig, poor

Brig. What has he done to you?" The shaggy little dog licked Marcy's hand as though he understood and appreciated her sympathy.

Kevin suggested that they try to put a splint on Brig's leg. "Darby, why don't you go back to where Jake surprised us and see if you can pick up some of the gold nuggets while I fix up Brigadoon."

Darby, disregarding the rocks and dirt falling around him, grabbed a flashlight and streaked back to the mine face, returning shortly with his pockets stuffed with gold ore. By this time Kevin had fashioned a rough splint from some pieces of the broken timbers, and Larry had tied a handkerchief about Jake's head to help stop the bleeding.

"How are we going to get him out of here?" asked Ramona. "He's too large for you to carry."

"My first thought is to leave him here," answered Larry, "but I know that wouldn't be right. I thought that you and I could each take hold under one arm and haul him out between us. It wouldn't be the best thing for him, but we can't help that."

Kevin and Marcy hurried ahead with a flashlight, gently carrying Brigadoon, while Darby brought up the rear. Larry and Ramona stopped frequently to rest their arms from the strain of Jake's dead weight. They were about ten yards from the entrance to the mine when a splintering crash from behind sent a cloud of choking dust billowing toward them.

"The mine's collapsing. We'll have to leave Jake here. It's either him or us," Larry yelled at Ramona as they both fell to coughing and sneezing. They eased Jake's body onto the mine floor and shouted to the others to run for the entrance. As they stumbled into the bright sunlight of the late afternoon, the mine continued to fall in upon itself.

Darby paused, looked back, and in a voice almost broken with grief cried, "The gold . . . we didn't get the gold."

Ramona grabbed Darby's arm, shoved him down the trail and spoke sharply, "Darby, this is no time to worry about the gold. Get moving! I think this whole mountainside is going to slide into the canyon."

All five of them scrambled down the trail as hastily as they could. Several times they stumbled into rocks, bruising their legs and arms. Marcy tumbled into a barrel cactus that left several sharp spines in her arm. A couple of times during their flight they paused to look behind them for a second or two. Ramona's prediction was indeed coming true—the entire mountainside was giving way. They had fled perhaps two hundred yards from the entrance to the mine when Marcy collapsed in a heap, crying, "I just can't go on. I'm staying here, no matter what happens."

Larry scooped Marcy into his arms and panted, "No you don't, little sister. We're not quite safe yet, but we don't have much farther to go." The battered hikers stumbled ahead another fifty yards up the canyon where Larry propped Marcy up against a small rock and then sank exhausted to the ground.

"There you go, Sis. I think we'll be O.K. here."

The dirty, sweaty five huddled together and watched the unbelievable happen. With the collapse of the mine, the next one hundred feet of cliff above it gave way and roared into the canyon. This, in turn, triggered several major landslides. Huge, truck-sized boulders thundered down from the cliffs on one side, rolled across the canyon, bounced off the opposite walls, and finally rolled back to come to rest at the bottom. Smaller rocks, trees, and cacti all came rumbling down in a blinding shower of dust and dirt to the floor of the valley and then rolled partway up the other side.

Gasping and choking from the dust, the young people covered their faces to help them continue breathing. At times it looked as though they would be swallowed by the landslide. One ricocheting rock left a welt on Kevin's head, and another slashed Larry's cheek, leaving a nasty, bleeding wound. Brigadoon whimpered partly from pain and partly from fear of the bedlam about him.

The devastating rockslide continued for several minutes. When the dust had settled somewhat, the hikers looked across the canyon and saw a completely different landscape. The entire rocky cliff had disappeared, while the mine entrance was buried beneath fifty feet of boulders and other rubble.

Larry carefully laid Brigadoon on the rocks, blew his nose, stood, and turned toward the Indian girl. "Ramona, you have been right each time you warned us about the dangers of looting the mine. Greedy people who invade your sacred lands in search of gold never seem to come out richer. Some never come out at all." Larry paused for a moment and then continued softly, "We were lucky. We escaped death by a few minutes. We found a gold mine—maybe the Lost Dutchman Mine, but it was ours only briefly. Once again, it has been returned to its rightful owners, your Apache Thunder Gods."

Ramona managed a weak smile and replied in a calm voice. "Several times on this trip I have prayed to my gods to bring us out of this alive. They did send us this thunderous warning, and they have guided us to safety. I believe it would be best if we now made a vow between us never to reveal that we ever found the mine. If we let others know, they will start a search for the gold. More pain and death will follow. Do you all agree? If you do, help me tell my gods what you have decided."

Ramona stood tall and invited the others to join her. All of them came slowly to their feet and grouped themselves about their quiet, darkskinned friend. She raised her arms, palms outstretched, to the sky and spoke in a clear voice that carried across the canyon. "Apache spirits, we thank you for keeping us from a terrible death. In exchange for our lives we agree never to tell where the gold is buried. We also pledge that we will never tell what happened to us today."

Ramona lowered her arms and stood quietly for several moments. The others stood with her, and although they said nothing, it was understood by all that they would hold sacred the vow they had promised Ramona's spiritual ancestors. Darby slowly emptied his pockets of the gold nuggets he had brought from the mine, and with all the strength he could muster, threw them into the rubble in the canyon.

19

BIG BIRD FROM THE SKY

One by one, without speaking, they turned their backs on the remains of the avalanche and began walking away single file. No one spoke. Even Brigadoon lay quietly with his muzzle in the crook of the Ohioan's arm, his soft brown eyes studying the surrounding terrain.

They were filled with their own thoughts of the events they had witnessed. Each seemed to know that much of what they had seen and taken part in would have to remain a secret among the five of them. Sensing this gave each a feeling of closeness with the others, and they seemed to be communicating this in their silence.

"I was just thinking," said Kevin, "it's strange that we should have gotten through all of the trouble we've had and escaped from the mine, and everything, and now here we are without any food or water."

"We'll never make it back to the jeep without food," moaned Marcy, her face white with fright and fatigue. "Everything—water, cans, map—all of it is under that landslide."

"She's right," Darby agreed. "Maybe we'd have been better off if we had stayed in the mine with Jake. They say death from thirst is an awful way to go. And I don't think starvation is much fun either."

Ramona, who had been in the lead, turned to face them. "The Apache gods have not let you down," she said. "They are no doubt pleased that each of you has taken a silent vow never to reveal anything about the mine. We have been spared for a purpose. The gods will see us safely out of the mountains."

"I wish I had your faith," said Larry, "but in this heat we're going to need water soon. We can't go on much longer."

"Look up above that cliff," said Ramona, pointing down the canyon.

Overhead, they saw great piles of thunderclouds moving in their direction. Darts of lightning flickered like snake tongues from one part of the clouds to another. For the first time, the hikers heard the rumble of thunder. Gusts of wind caused whirling funnels of dust to spiral high above the canyon floor. Violent updrafts within the clouds caused them to change form, and Darby wondered if his imagination was playing tricks or if he really saw faces of the Apache gods among the billowy shapes.

"We'll soon have lots of water," said Ramona. "At least enough to keep us going until we can find a spring."

While she was speaking, the winds gusted more strongly and the young people pressed against the flat face of a large rock for protection against the sharp sting of the tiny sand grains. As the clouds closed in overhead, the bright sunlight gave way to an eerie twilight and finally to a gloomy darkness. Tremendous lightning discharges jumped about the sky in jagged, neonlike displays, lighting up the black clouds briefly. Claps of thunder rolled over the hikers in waves of deafening noise. Quickly, the sky let loose a cloudburst that drenched the thirsty party and the parched desert about them. The rain, driven by the wind, blew over the mountains in great flowing sheets that partly hid the towering cliffs and made them seem like great sailing ships being blown across a vast ocean.

As they watched, the five of them welcomed the great cold drops that soaked their clothes and dripped from their hair. They stood with their mouths open, letting the rain splatter directly onto their tongues. Drenched, they danced in a circle, laughing and stomping in the puddles that formed around them. Finally exhausted, they sank to the ground, panting.

"The rain is great," said Larry, "but it is presenting a new danger."

"I know," answered Ramona, "flash floods."

"You're right," replied Larry. "That water will really come rolling down some of these arroyos. We're all right here, but we'd better not try to move for an hour or so after the rain stops."

Nearly as abruptly as it had begun, the storm ceased, and the revived adventurers settled down for a rest. They watched muddy streams from ravines join to produce a torrent of water that swept through the canyon.

Almost an hour later, the sun was out again, and the temperature had risen to what seemed nearly a hundred.

"We should be able to find pools of water for part of the return trip from the rain that your Apache gods provided," said Larry, "but I wonder if they will be so quick to answer our need for food."

Larry had barely finished his sentence when Brig began to growl and stare up the canyon. As they all stood watching, a water-soaked burro came into view around the bend in the trail, sloshing through the mud left in the wake of the flash flood. The animal was laden with packs, some of which looked familiar to the hikers as the burro approached.

"It's Jake's burro!" said Marcy.

"And the Apache gods have sent us food!" marveled Larry, his eyes wide with wonder.

An hour later the five adventurers were dragging through the mud on the trail. They had unloaded the burro and set it free to join the others of its kind that ran wild in the mountains. Papers they found in the saddlebags on the animal showed that Jake was indeed Jacob Walz, but there was nothing to prove that he was the grandson of the famous Dutchman. What looked like a diary written in German, Larry tucked into his knapsack, hoping someday to have it translated. A few German coins were divided among the other members of the party.

As they moved along, talking among themselves, Larry suddenly raised his hand. "Quiet!" he shouted. "I think I hear something."

The others listened.

"What is it?" Ramona asked.

"It's some kind of engine," Larry replied.

Suddenly, all of them could hear it.

"It's a helicopter!" shouted Kevin, who was now carrying Brig. "They're probably looking for us."

"Give me one of those tin cans," said Larry. "I'm going to see if I can reflect some light off the lid. Maybe I can get their attention. The rest of you wave your bandannas and jump up and down!"

The helicopter came into view, heading directly toward them. Frantically, Larry moved the can back and forth, trying to reflect the rays of the sun into the helicopter. About three hundred yards before it reached them, the aircraft suddenly veered and headed into a canyon that cut into the mountainside.

"Oh, no," moaned Darby. "They didn't see us."

The group sat down wearily, their exuberance drained by their disappointment.

"So near and yet so far," said Ramona.

Suddenly Marcy jumped to her feet. "Here he comes again," she shouted.

This time the pilot saw them. As he hovered overhead, the hikers began to look for a place where the airship could land.

"How about over there in that small clearing?" asked Kevin.

"Yeah, let's go," said Darby. "He sees it too."

Sometime later, Larry, Marcy, and Brigadoon waited with Mr. and Mrs. Coleman at a temporary ranger station that had been set up at Goldfields.

The Colemans, upon returning from Hawaii and finding the children gone, had instigated the helicopter search that morning with the help of the forest rangers. When the young people had finally been located, it had been agreed that Larry should go out first because of the cut on his face. Since Marcy was the youngest, she had been sent along, feeling very much like Florence Nightingale as she fussed over Larry and Brigadoon.

Marcy and Larry had agreed that they would make no statement until the others had been picked up and brought out of the Superstitions. Now, with their parents, two rangers, and a deputy sheriff, they eagerly awaited the others' arrival.

When the helicopter landed, there was another joyful reunion. Ramona, after watching the others being warmly greeted, began to make an apology for taking Marcy, Kevin, and Darby into the Superstitions, but the Colemans quieted her and drew her into the family circle with loving hugs and tender pats.

"You're all back safe and pretty sound," said Mrs. Coleman. "Right now, that's all that matters."

The newspapers the next day carried the story of how five young people and a dog had escaped death when a mine they were exploring caved in. The young people had seen an old man with a burro earlier, but they had seen only the burro after the landslide. In the newspaper account the forest rangers speculated that probably the man was killed during the cave-in. The stories gave no clues to the location of the mine, nor was there any mention of the treasure they had seen. Also not referred to were the events leading up to the discovery of the mine and Jake's attempts to kill them.

Another story in the same issue of the newspaper told of the arrest of twelve prospectors who had been apprehended in the Superstitions on various charges including illegal blasting and falsified mining claims. The story stated that one of the miners, a woman who had formerly sung with the San Francisco opera, had been charged with murder.

"Well, I finally see what you meant when you said, 'Not bad shooting for an opera singer,'" said Darby to his oldest cousin.

Larry laughed. "She was a real character," he said. "She had some big plan that if she could strike it rich, she could revive her career. She had a strong voice all right, but I'm afraid it had seen better days."

"Hey!" exclaimed Kevin, who was studying the newspaper. "Did you see this story where they found a cactus wearing a red hat?"

Marcy joined the others in laughter as they remembered the fate of Darby's headgear on their way into the mountains.

"He's just kidding you," she told Darby, "but it was kinda funny wasn't it?"

"Yeah," laughed Darby, "I have to admit that saguaro did look pretty silly wearing my hat."

Later, the five friends took a final walk together in the

warm spring evening. The last rays of the setting sun struck just the top of the Superstitions, setting aglow the light-colored rocks. A lone thunderhead towered above the mountains. Suddenly there were flashes of lightning from the cloud to the mountain top. The five friends stopped and watched the display and listened to the thunder which rolled in gently from the distance.

Darby spoke quietly. "Two weeks ago I would have said, 'Look at the lightning.' It wouldn't have been a big deal. This evening, it's very different. I feel that perhaps the Thunder Gods are again speaking to me. I wonder what they are saying?"

"Who knows for sure?" Ramona said. "They probably are thanking us for keeping faith with them. In any case, I would like you to be my guest on the reservation. Kevin and Marcy will be there. Do you think you can make your way out here next summer?"

"I'll sure try," Darby said with determination.

Although no one spoke, everyone seemed to be moved by the same feeling. They gathered closer, clasped hands, and stood silently for perhaps a minute. Their eyes pledged deep friendship and understanding for years ahead. Dropping hands, they quietly walked back to the house as night closed about them, and a final peal of thunder echoed back from Wee-Kit-Saur-Ah.

TO OUR READERS

Many of the happenings and all of the people in this story are just imaginings to entertain you. There was no Jake, and the boys and girls he treated so badly do not exist.

There are many true things about this story, however. Don Peralta was massacred in the Superstition Mountains in 1847 as he was bringing out gold. There was a German named Walz who claimed to have discovered the old Peralta mines. The old "Dutchman" died without telling others about the location of the gold. Police have on their records unsolved murders of people who went into the mountains to find the Lost Dutchman Mine.

If there was ever a rich gold deposit, it has never been found, and many of the crimes committed in the mountains have never been solved. Although one can never be sure, perhaps in the Superstitions dwell Apache gods who stand guard over any gold that might be buried there. It may be that those who violate the spiritual home of the Apaches are punished by hardship and death.